W9-ALN-150

THE FIVE ANCESTORS
OUT OF THE ASHES
Book 2

LION

The Five Ancestors

The Five Ancestors
OUT OF THE ASHES

THE FIVE ANCESTORS
OUT OF THE ASHES
Book 2

LION

JEFF STONE

Random House 🏠 New York

Text copyright © 2013 by Jeffrey S. Stone
Jacket art copyright © 2013 by Richard Cowdrey

All rights reserved. Published in the United States by Random House Children's Books, a division of Random House, Inc., New York.

Random House and the colophon are registered trademarks of Random House, Inc. The Five Ancestors is a registered trademark of Jeffrey S. Stone.

Visit us on the Web! randomhouse.com/kids

Educators and librarians, for a variety of teaching tools, visit us at RHTeachersLibrarians.com

Library of Congress Cataloging-in-Publication Data
Stone, Jeff.
Lion / Jeff Stone. — 1st ed.
p. cm. — (Five ancestors: out of the ashes ; bk. 2)
Summary: Betrayed by his uncle, Dr. V., Ryan must rely on his friends to help him recover and rebuild his life but Dr. V's confederates think the four friends still know too much and follow them to California to silence them.
ISBN 978-0-375-87019-4 (trade) — ISBN 978-0-375-97019-1 (lib. bdg.) —
ISBN 978-0-375-98760-1 (ebook)
[1. Bicycles and bicycling—Fiction. 2. Bicycle racing—Fiction. 3. Adventure and adventurers—Fiction. 4. Supernatural—Fiction. 5. Chinese Americans—Fiction. 6. California—Fiction.] I. Title.
PZ7.S87783Lio 2013   [Fic]—dc23   2013004945

Printed in the United States of America
10 9 8 7 6 5 4 3 2 1
First Edition

For Keith Boggs,
book-loving sensei

THE FIVE ANCESTORS
OUT OF THE ASHES
Book 2

LION

STAGE ONE

PELOTON:

The main group of riders,
also known as a "pack"

"You can do it, Ryan!" Phoenix Collins shouted from above me.

I gritted my teeth. Of course I could do it. If Phoenix could do it, so could I.

I shifted my mountain bike into an easier gear and inched up the muddy slope. Two feet forward, one foot back. Two more feet forward, one and a half feet back. It was quickly becoming an impossible climb. The already heavy rain was getting worse, sending rivers of brown water down the troughs that the other three bikes had gouged into the hillside ahead of me. Strange-smelling sweat poured from beneath my helmet, mixing with the warm July rain.

"Dig deep, bro!" Jake called down.

"Push yourself!" Hú Dié shouted.

My thighs burned and my calves ached, but I continued to hammer, my legs pumping like pistons. My riding shoes were connected to my pedals, and my quads bulged on the upstroke, my large hamstrings working the downstroke.

I roared like the lion on my Vanderhausen family's Belgian coat of arms.

"Whoo-hoo!" Hú Dié called out. "That is the spirit!"

I looked up to see that I was nearing the top of the hill, where Phoenix, Jake, and Hú Dié were waiting for me on this training ride.

"Almost there!" Phoenix called out. "You're doing great!"

I frowned. I knew Phoenix was only trying to help, trying to motivate me to sweat a dangerous substance called dragon bone from my system. But some of his comments were beginning to get on my nerves. The last thing a guy in last place wants to hear is how great he's doing.

"Come on, Ryan!" Phoenix shouted. "If you manage to catch me, I'll—"

"Arrr!" I growled, and I drove my legs even harder.

My bike began to fishtail, the rear tire swinging wildly from side to side. I rose out of the saddle and shifted my weight back over the rear tire. Mud and trail debris sprayed up around me while massive raindrops pelted my helmet. I couldn't see a thing.

I felt an unexpected jolt as my front tire bumped over a gnarled tree root, and my slipping rear tire found an instant of traction. There was a sudden increase in torque against my drive sprocket and—

SNAP!

My bike chain broke in half.

My legs began to free-spin wildly. I started to slide backward, and I cut my wheel to one side. The bike spun around as I'd hoped, but it went too far. I'd only wanted it to turn ninety degrees so that I could ditch the bike on a downhill angle. Instead, it did a complete one-eighty.

I found myself barreling straight down the muddy slope, my legs still whirling. I tapped the brake levers, but it was no use. There was too much mud and gunk lodged in the calipers.

I slowed my spinning legs and saw rows of gnarled scrub pine waiting for me at the bottom of the hill, their dagger-like arms outstretched. I disconnected one foot and cut the wheel again, jamming my mountain bike shoe into the hillside. The bike began to slow, but then my foot skittered across a slick rocky shelf and I lost control.

I dropped onto my side, quickly disconnecting my other foot and kicking the bike away from me as my leg, hip, and rib cage scraped over the exposed rock like raw meat across a cheese grater. I opened my mouth to cry out in pain, but my torso collided with the base of a large oak tree and all the air was forced out of my lungs.

My momentum continued to push me around the tree, and I rolled a few more feet before finally coming to a stop. I closed my eyes, struggling to catch my breath. The muscles of my abdomen began to cramp, but they relaxed a moment later, to my great relief. When I opened my eyes again, I saw that I was at the bottom of the hill, just a few feet in front of the wicked scrub pines. My bike was about ten feet away, half buried in mud and pine needles.

From the top of the hill, Phoenix called out, "We'll be right down, Ryan! Sit tight!"

I didn't feel like sitting around for anybody. I stood on

wobbly legs and checked myself over. My rib cage and one of my legs were sore and scraped up, and my riding jersey was mud-streaked and torn. Otherwise, I seemed to be okay.

I couldn't say the same about my bike. I walked over to it and saw that it was trashed. It was a prototype frame made of sturdy lightweight magnesium. Apparently, it wasn't sturdy enough. The frame was cracked in at least three spots. Also, the rear stays were bent and the handlebars were twisted. My rich uncle, the recently deceased Dr. V, had paid twelve grand for this thing, and it was unrideable after one wreck. What a piece of junk. A horrible bike from a horrible man.

Phoenix, Jake, and Hú Dié slid down to me. They'd left their bikes and helmets at the top of the hill. Phoenix's freaky green Chinese eyes shone brightly in the gloom, his weird reddish hair glistening in the rain.

"Are you okay?" he asked.

"I'm fine," I replied.

"Bro, you don't look fine," Jake said.

I shook my head. Jake had a habit of blurting out whatever popped into his head. Sometimes it was amusing. Other times, not so much.

I glared at him.

Jake took a step back, flipping a clump of wet, shaggy blond hair out of his face. He raised his hands. "Easy, man. I'm just joking. Don't Hulk out on me or anything."

"I don't *Hulk out*," I said.

"No? You roared and snapped your chain like it was a rubber band."

"I guess I don't know my own strength." I shrugged and turned away.

"Ryan!" Hú Dié said suddenly. "Your side! You are bleeding badly."

I twisted and looked at my left side—the side that had absorbed the impact as I slid over the rocks. My torn jersey was still coated with mud, but the mud was now mixed with a deep red.

Phoenix stepped close to me and peered through the rip in my riding jersey. He grimaced. "Doesn't it hurt?"

I shrugged. "It hurt when it happened, but not anymore."

"Maybe you are in shock," Hú Dié said. "We should go."

"Hang on," I said. "I want to see. I thought it was just some minor scrapes." I took off my shirt and let the rain wash over my wounds. It stung a little, causing my chest and back muscles to ripple.

Hú Dié looked away, apparently embarrassed.

I grinned. I'd tried to get her to look at my fine physique once before, but she'd laughed at me. She was one of the prettiest girls I'd ever seen.

Jake smacked my arm. "That's enough, Beefcake. You'd better cover up. Those cuts won't coagulate with water pouring all over them. Let the rain rinse some of the mud off your shirt, then wring it out and tie it around yourself."

"Look," Phoenix said, staring at my side.

I followed Phoenix's gaze to a cut that seemed much deeper than the rest. It was like watching time-lapse photography. It appeared to be healing from the inside amazingly fast.

"Whoa!" Jake said. "What was in your cornflakes this morning?"

I didn't reply. The rapid healing must have had

something to do with the dragon bone in my system—this ancient Chinese herb my uncle had given me as a performance enhancer. Phoenix and Hú Dié knew all about it, but Jake didn't. We wanted to keep it that way.

Hú Dié glanced at my healing wound but said nothing.

Phoenix straightened. "Let's head back to my house. I want my uncle Tí to see this." Phoenix's uncle was a doctor, and he'd been studying dragon bone.

"Forget that!" Jake said. "Let's go to *my* house so that we can grab my camera. You'll be a YouTube sensation!"

"No," I said. "No video."

Jake frowned. "Why not?"

"Because I said so."

"What's going on?" Jake asked.

"Nothing," I replied. "It's not a big deal."

"What did your uncle do to you?"

"He didn't do anything, Jake."

"Seriously, bro. You go to live with your drug guru uncle for like six months, and when you come back you're the most ripped kid on the planet. Now you're healing like a mutant. What gives?"

I felt my face darken. "The only things my uncle ever gave me were vitamins and all-natural herbal supplements. I don't know what's going on with this cut, but my six-pack came from working out a *ton*. That's all I did when I was with my uncle besides ride. It's not like I had any friends. You guys stopped talking to me after my dad died, remember?"

"Come on, man," Jake said. "Don't be that way. You moved thousands of miles away from us."

"You could have emailed or Skyped."

"Uh—"

"Forget about it," I said. "I understand why you guys might have thought I didn't want to hang with you anymore. I'm over it, and I hope you are, too. Just don't push me about this stuff, all right? It really bugs me."

"Sure," Jake said. He made a fist and raised his knuckles toward me. "Bros?"

I made a fist, bumping it with Jake's. "Bros," I said. "And for the record, I'm glad we're all friends again, including Hú Dié."

Hú Dié smiled. "Me too."

Phoenix raised a fist and we bumped, but he didn't say a word.

I wrung out most of the mud from my shirt; then I pressed it against my side while Phoenix grabbed my bike, and the four of us trudged up the slippery slope.

We reached the trailhead of Town Run Trail Park to find the parking lot completely submerged. Hú Dié and Jake pushed their bikes through the ankle-deep quagmire while I waded behind them, still pressing my shirt against my side. Phoenix pushed his bike with one hand and carried my battered bike over his shoulder.

There was a crew-cab pickup truck idling off to one side of the parking lot. A man wearing a dripping-wet poncho climbed out of the driver's seat. He waved.

Hú Dié removed a slender tire pump from her bike frame. She gripped it like a club.

"Relax," I said to her. "It's Smitty. He's the trail supervisor. He's cool."

"Oh," Hú Dié said, but she didn't put the pump back.

"Phoenix!" Smitty called out. "Ryan! Jake! How goes it?"

"Slow and wet, Smitty," Phoenix replied. "Ryan took a spill."

Smitty sloshed over to us. "Are you okay, big man? Let me see."

"I'm fine," I said. "Really."

"I'll be the judge of that. Show me the damage."

I reluctantly pulled my shirt away and was shocked to see that most of my cuts were now basically just scratches. The deep wound was little more than a scab.

Smitty laughed. "Seriously, Ryan? If you wanted to take off your shirt to impress the young lady, you could have come up with a better excuse than those scuff marks."

Hú Dié smiled, and I shook out my shirt. As I put it back on, the rain slowed to a drizzle.

Smitty turned to Hú Dié. "Hi. My name is Scott Smith, but everybody calls me Smitty."

"Pleased to meet you, Smitty," she said. "My name is Hú Dié."

"Hoo-DEE-ay?" Smitty asked.

"Yes," Hú Dié said, sounding surprised. "You pronounced it perfectly."

"Thanks. I studied some Chinese in college. Does your name mean *Metal Butterfly*?"

"Close," she said. "It means *Iron* Butterfly."

"Great name. Appropriate, too. You're the girl who trounced all the fourteen-year-old guys at last Saturday's mountain bike race, aren't you?"

"Yes."

"Trounced?" Jake said. "She didn't finish *that* far ahead of me."

Smitty laughed again. "You got beat by a girl, Jake. Ten yards or ten miles, it really doesn't matter."

Jake stuck his lip out.

"So, how's the trail?" Smitty asked.

"Not good," Phoenix answered. "We tore up the last hill pretty bad, and the rest of the trail is washing out quickly, too."

"I figured it must be bad when I saw you carrying Ryan's bike. Have you guys seen the weather forecast?"

All four of us shook our heads.

"It's supposed to rain like this for the next few days," Smitty said. "Most of the other supervisors around here have closed their trails. I'm going to close this one, too."

"When will it reopen?" Hú Dié asked.

"Hard to say. The White River bordering us is bound to overflow its banks. It always does. Once it stops raining and the water recedes, it will take about a week for the trail to dry out. Then it will take another few weeks of evenings and weekends for our volunteers to repair whatever damage the river and rain cause. Trails are a lot of work."

"So it might be an entire *month* before anyone can ride here again?" Hú Dié asked.

"It might," Smitty said. "Some of the other trails in the area could take longer. They have fewer volunteers than we do."

Hú Dié glanced at me. I needed to sweat, and she knew it. Mountain biking was going to help break my bond with dragon bone.

"What about the summer mountain bike racing series?" Phoenix asked.

"It's not looking good," Smitty said. "There's a phone conference about it tonight, but I wouldn't be surprised if we canceled it."

"Oh, no," Hú Dié said. "We were hoping to ride our mountain bikes a lot over the rest of summer vacation. I actually just built this one yesterday from some of Phoenix's old parts. I only have a limited amount of time before I have to go back home to China."

"I'm sorry," Smitty said. "It might not be so bad for you, though, Hú Dié. The first race of the season didn't count because Ryan was the only one to finish. We've only had one other race since, and you won it. You might just end up being our series grand champion."

"I do not care about that," Hú Dié said. "I just want to be able to ride."

"If the four of you scrounge up some rakes and shovels, you can join the trail maintenance team," Smitty offered. "The more help we have, the sooner we'll all get to ride."

"Great," Phoenix said. "Keep us posted. Thanks, Smitty."

"No problem. I'm going to lock the gate now. How are you all getting home?"

"We were going to ride," Phoenix said, glancing at my ruined bike, "but we can walk. The rain has almost stopped, and my house is only a couple miles from here."

"How about a lift?" Smitty said. "I've got room for your bikes in my truck bed, and we can all pile into the cab. My pickup has two rows of seats."

"Thanks for the offer," I said, "but we're soaking wet and muddy."

"So am I," Smitty said. "Besides, the inside of my truck is dirtier than you all. Let's go."

• • •

Jake asked to be dropped off at his house instead of going to Phoenix's. He didn't have a change of clothes, but my mom had dropped off a set for me at Phoenix's house while we were riding. I'd planned to spend the whole day with Phoenix and Hú Dié, and I was secretly glad that Jake wouldn't be hanging out with us because it meant that Phoenix, Hú Dié, and I could talk openly about dragon bone with Phoenix's grandfather and his uncle Tí.

After dropping off Jake, Phoenix navigated Smitty down a few side streets until we were on a road that was surprisingly rural for being in the middle of a city. I only saw three gravel driveways, and Phoenix told us where to turn. The drive was long and winding, with trees lining it the whole way. You couldn't even see the house from the road. It was cool. I'd never been there before.

The driveway led to a small house that wasn't even a quarter the size of mine. Phoenix's grandfather's old Ford Ranger pickup was parked in front. Beside the truck was a car I didn't recognize.

"Looks like my uncle Tí is still here," Phoenix said.

Smitty parked beside the Ranger and we climbed out. We unloaded the bikes and thanked Smitty for the ride.

"My pleasure," Smitty said. "Chauffeuring you guys around reminded me how much I need to clean out my truck."

"No worries," Phoenix said. "Thanks for the lift."

"See you at the trail clean-ups?" Smitty asked.

"I hope so," Phoenix said.

We waved, and Smitty drove off.

"Let's put the bikes on the back porch," Phoenix said.

Hú Dié and I followed him around to the rear of the

house. The rain had lessened a lot, and I could hear the White River rushing nearby beyond a wall of trees.

"This place is awesome," I said.

"Thanks," Phoenix said. "We have several acres. The house is kind of small, though."

"It is not," Hú Dié argued. "It is much bigger than most apartments in China, including ours. I just love all these trees and the river. It is perfect." She turned to me. "Maybe now you understand why I chose to stay here, although I appreciate your mother's offer to let me stay with you until my travel visa expires."

"I totally get it," I said. "Have you always lived here, Phoenix?"

"Yes. My parents bought this place before I was born. I'm glad Grandfather chose to stay here after that stupid car wreck."

"It is so great that your grandfather moved from China to take care of you," Hú Dié said.

"Yeah," Phoenix said. "Grandfather can be grumpy sometimes, but he's still the best."

We reached the long rear porch, and the back door opened. A middle-aged Chinese man poked his head out.

"Hi, Uncle Tí!" I said. Phoenix's uncle had been helping me with my dragon bone dependency, and I'd spent so much time with him lately that I also called him Uncle. So did Hú Dié.

"Hello, Uncle Tí," Hú Dié said.

"The gang's all here!" Uncle Tí said. "Come on in. I'm making fish head soup. Lots of collagen. Good for your joints."

I cringed.

We took off our muddy shoes and wet socks, and Uncle Tí tossed us some towels. We wiped off as best we could and went inside.

We were in the kitchen, where a large pot simmered on the stovetop. It smelled *good*. However, I couldn't bring myself to peer inside the pot like Phoenix and Hú Dié were doing.

"Have a seat," Uncle Tí said. "Lunch will be ready in about half an hour. I'll try to wake Grandfather now. He's due to get up, anyway."

Phoenix looked at me. "*Grandfather* is a Chinese term of endearment. My grandfather is actually Uncle Tí's father."

Uncle Tí nodded.

"Sure," I said, not believing a word.

I'd heard from *my* uncle that Phoenix's "grandfather" was actually more like his great-great-great-great-grandfather. Supposedly, he was close to four hundred years old. I never would have believed it if I hadn't taken dragon bone. That stuff defied description. In my case, it gave me extra strength and stamina when I took large amounts of it, and now it seemed that it also healed wounds incredibly fast. My uncle claimed that a person could take it for a short time without any complications, but if someone took it for a long time, other factors would kick in. Mainly, the dragon bone would extend a person's life indefinitely, like it apparently had with Phoenix's grandfather. However, if the person ever stopped taking it, he would die.

Some guys had stolen Phoenix's grandfather's supply of dragon bone, and he would have died if Phoenix hadn't gotten it back. I'd heard that Phoenix's grandfather was still in pretty bad shape, trying to recover from having been without it.

Uncle Tí returned, leading Phoenix's grandfather by the arm, and I had a hard time looking at the old man. He was very tall and slender, and he normally stood ramrod straight. Now he hobbled forward, hunched over and shaky. His skin was gray and flaking, like a shedding reptile, and his previously long, thick hair had thinned. It hung in limp strands around his neck and shoulders. He glanced over at me, and I saw that at least his eyes were still clear and bright.

"I'm a mess, aren't I, Ryan?" Phoenix's grandfather asked in a hoarse whisper.

"Ah . . ." I didn't know what to say.

"No need to answer," he continued. "Your reaction says it all. This is what dragon bone does to a person. Do not let it take root in you, or it will steal all of your *chi*—your life energy. But you already know this, don't you?"

I nodded. "Uncle Tí told me. I do have less energy than usual, but sweating seems to help."

"Very good. How is your stomach?"

"You mean my abdominal muscles? They still cramp up sometimes."

"You know why that is, don't you?"

"Yes. The dragon bone concentrates in my *dan tien*, my *chi* center. It's the spot where a person feels 'butterflies' in their stomach."

"That is correct. Think of dragon bone as a living thing. In its powdered form, it is dormant. But once consumed, it awakens and resides inside you. Your *dan tien* is its home.

The more you take, the stronger it becomes. It rewards you by making you stronger in a number of ways. Unfortunately, when you do not feed it, it retaliates by hurting you. It squeezes your abdominal muscles and begins to siphon your *chi* from throughout your body. As you continue to wean yourself from it, your cramping may spread to other parts of your body as the dragon bone attempts to make you feed it more. It will hurt like no pain you have ever experienced. Do not give in."

"I won't."

"I hope not. The dragon bone within me is fighting for more, but I am a stubborn old man, and I refuse to give it more than half the amount I used to. I will no longer let it push me around without me pushing back."

I swallowed hard.

"Do you have any questions?" Phoenix's grandfather asked.

"No," I said, "but I want to show you and Uncle Tí something."

I pulled off my shirt and turned my left side toward Phoenix's grandfather. "See these scrapes? Less than an hour ago, many of them were bleeding cuts. The deepest one healed before our very eyes. I hardly even felt any pain after I was first hurt."

"A reduction in pain can be expected," Phoenix's grandfather said, "as can accelerated healing in certain circumstances. How deep were the cuts?"

"Much deeper than what you see," Phoenix answered. "The worst one was bleeding everywhere one minute, then it wasn't. I saw it with my own eyes. The wound repaired itself from the inside out. Just look at his shirt. That big stain isn't mud."

"I want to see those wounds," Uncle Tí said. He washed his hands in the kitchen sink and began to examine my side with his fingers. "I don't see any sign of accelerated healing."

"I guess it stopped once it got to this point," I said. "The scrapes look exactly the same now as they did when we left the trail park."

"I have seen this phenomenon before," Phoenix's grandfather said. "It has even happened to me on occasion. The dragon bone rushes to heal a major wound until it is no longer a threat to its host's survival. The process often heals lesser wounds at the same time. Who else witnessed this?"

"I did," Hú Dié said. "So did Jake."

Uncle Tí looked concerned. "Jake? How did he react?"

"He kind of flipped out," Phoenix said. "Fortunately, he believes Ryan's uncle is behind it. He thinks Dr. V pumped Ryan full of experimental chemicals."

Phoenix's grandfather rubbed his long chin. "I suppose that may be our best explanation, if we should ever need one. We cannot let the truth get out."

I took a deep breath. "I . . . um . . . there's something I need to tell you."

Phoenix's grandfather's eyes narrowed and he glared at me. He looked just like a snake. "What?"

"The truth may already be out."

Everyone was looking at me.

"I didn't *do* anything!" I quickly said. "I'm just passing along information. The police in Texas contacted my mother last night. They still can't find Lin Tan."

I saw Hú Dié's eyes widen while Phoenix scowled. I knew I had to be careful with what I said next. Hú Dié had double-crossed Phoenix with Lin Tan in an attempt to steal some dragon bone. At the last minute, however, she stuck with Phoenix, even taking a bullet for him. However, Lin Tan was still a sore subject between them.

"What are the details?" Phoenix's grandfather asked.

"There aren't any, really," I said, "other than the fact that they can't find him. My uncle shot him in the chest, but he still managed to kill Murphy and then get away without a trace. I've been thinking about how my wounds healed so quickly and—"

"And you believe Lin Tan might be taking dragon bone," Phoenix said.

"Yeah."

Phoenix's grandfather nodded slowly. "That is possible. Did you ever *see* him take it?"

"No," I said, "but he's the one who delivered it to my uncle down there. Maybe he set some aside for himself."

"We have to find him," Phoenix said.

"We will never find him," Hú Dié said. "He knows many people in many countries. He is a popular road bike and cyclocross racer with many . . . connections."

"Are you sticking up for him?" Phoenix asked.

"No. His connections are questionable."

"That's putting it mildly," I said. "He's currently suspended for using steroids."

Uncle Tí turned to Phoenix. "Hú Dié is right. Lin Tan is beyond our reach. If the police can't find him, we won't be able to. Besides, even if we did find him, what could we do?"

"I've got a thousand different kung fu moves that come to mind," Phoenix mumbled. "Who cares if he knows kung fu, too?"

Uncle Tí sighed. "I'll talk with PawPaw in Beijing. If any rumors begin to spread about dragon bone, she'll hear them."

"And I'll keep an eye on the Internet for anything that looks suspicious," I said. "I'm pretty good with computers."

"Very well," Uncle Tí said. "In the meantime, let's stay focused on the things that we *can* control. How was your ride today, Ryan? Do you think you're ready to reduce the amount of dragon bone you've been taking again?"

I shrugged. "Maybe. It depends on whether or not I can figure out a different way to sweat. All of the mountain bike trails around here will be closed for a while because of the weather."

"There are plenty of other ways to exercise," Uncle Tí said. "You appear to have spent enough time in the gym to know that."

"It's not the same," I said. "I sweat when I lift weights, but not like I do when I ride. I need to do something more aerobic."

"How about jogging?" Hú Dié suggested.

"I *hate* running," I said. "Besides, it's supposed to rain hard for days, remember?"

"What about the rec center in town?" Phoenix asked. "They have an indoor track, and an indoor swimming pool, too."

"No running," I said. "And I can't swim."

"Hmm . . . ," Phoenix said. "What about spinning? You could ride an exercise bike or buy an indoor trainer to connect to one of your bikes."

I shook my head. "I'd go crazy riding a bike for hours in the same spot."

Phoenix rolled his eyes.

"Why don't you learn kung fu?" Phoenix's grandfather suggested.

My eyebrows rose. "Kung fu?"

"That's a great idea," Uncle Tí said. "Phoenix could teach you. He's taken over Grandfather's tai chi class at the

THE FIVE ANCESTORS OUT OF THE ASHES

nursing home where I work, and he's proven to be an excellent instructor."

"Maybe," I said. "I've always wanted to learn kung fu."

"Kung fu is about much more than fighting," Uncle Tí said.

"I know. I've seen lots of kung fu movies. I've also seen old people in the park doing tai chi, and they didn't throw a single punch. Tai chi is kung fu, right?"

"It is," Hú Dié said. "Those old people you saw? They were throwing all kinds of punches and kicks. They just did it very *slow.*"

"Really?" I said.

"Really."

"I'm not sure about this," Phoenix said.

"I am," Hú Dié said. "It sounds fun. I can teach Ryan, too. Phoenix has seen my kung fu."

Phoenix shook his head. "Now I'm *really* not sure about this."

Hú Dié punched him in the arm. Hard.

"Ouch!" Phoenix yelped. "I've asked you before to stop doing that. When are you going to listen to me?"

"Never," Hú Dié said. "This is no longer about you. It is about Ryan now. Come on, we are going to teach Beefcake how to use his muscles for something other than posing." She walked to the other side of the kitchen and opened a door that led to the attached garage.

Uncle Tí looked at me. "Beefcake?"

I shook my head. "Don't ask."

"I'll be there in a minute," Phoenix said. "I want to get out of these wet clothes."

"Do not forget to do your hair and makeup," Hú Dié said. "Looking your best is important for exercising."

Phoenix groaned and turned to me. "You have no idea what you've just gotten yourself into." He headed off down a short hallway.

Uncle Tí laughed. "Go easy on Ryan, Hú Dié. Remember, we're going to eat lunch soon. And Ryan, the clothes your mother dropped off are in the bathroom. Feel free to change anytime."

I looked at Hú Dié. "Shouldn't we change, too?"

"You can sweat in your clean clothes or in your dirty ones," she said. "It is up to you. If you do change, do not put on socks. We practice kung fu barefoot. I am going to wait until we eat to change."

"I'll wait, too, then," I said.

Hú Dié nodded, and I followed her into the attached garage. She flipped on the lights.

"Whoa," I said.

Hú Dié closed the door. "I know."

The garage had been converted into a full-blown martial arts studio. Mirrors lined one wall, and the floor was covered with wrestling mats. A speed bag hung in the far corner, along with three different-sized heavy punch/kick bags. In another corner were items I'd only seen in kung fu movies. One was a man-sized wooden practice dummy that looked like a tree trunk with stubby branches poking out of it called a *mook jong*. Another was a *makiwara* board, basically a thick board wrapped with coarse rope that you punch in order to toughen your fists.

Then there were the mirrorless walls. They were lined

with racks of weapons. Some of the weapons were made of plastic or foam, clearly designed for practice. However, most had blades that looked sharp enough to shave with. I saw spears with different tips, as well as a bunch of swords. There were knives, nunchuks, whip chains, *sai, kwan daos,* triple staffs, bo staffs, short sticks, long sticks, walking sticks, canes, and a fan made of knife blades. There was even a flute carved out of bamboo and reinforced with metal rings that looked strong enough to cave someone's head in.

"This is kind of creepy," I said.

"I thought the same thing," Hú Dié said. "It is like Phoenix's grandfather is training him to singlehandedly fight an army."

"Why?"

"I do not know. I saw a few things in China with him at an old temple, but . . ." Her voice trailed off.

"But you're not supposed to talk about it," I said. "I understand. I'm getting used to their family secrets."

"There is nothing wrong with keeping secrets," Hú Dié said. "It is often safer to not know things than to know them, especially when it comes to someone else's personal business."

"I won't argue with that. I wish I'd never gotten wrapped up in Phoenix's family secrets and this dragon bone mess. I want to move on with my bike racing."

"Let us see what we can do about it, then. Once you learn even a little kung fu, you will become a better rider."

"You think?"

"I know. How do you think Phoenix became such a good rider?"

"By riding a lot."

"Does he ride a lot?"

I thought about it for a minute. "Not really."

"I have not known him long," Hú Dié said, "but I agree. He seems to ride just enough to stay ahead of everyone else. If someone or something is not pushing him, he appears to be lazy. If you learn half the kung fu he knows, you will beat him on a bicycle."

"I don't know. A big part of the reason I started taking dragon bone in the first place was so that I could beat Phoenix. You've seen where that's gotten me."

Hú Dié shook her head. "Phoenix's big advantage is the core strength he has developed doing martial arts. That is also why elite cyclists do yoga. He is skilled, for sure, and he could become a pro one day, but so could you. You could be better than him."

"That's not what my uncle said."

"Do you *remember* your uncle, Ryan? Why would you believe a word he said?"

I shrugged.

"I think that you work harder than anyone I have ever met," Hú Dié said. "And you have so much strength. People say that cycling is all about power-to-weight ratio, but that is not always true. Sometimes, it is *all* about power."

"Wow," I said. "That's what I think, too."

Hú Dié grinned. "Great alike minds. Now, how much martial arts training have you had?"

I chuckled. "None."

"Did you not learn the basics in school?"

"Heck, no. Did you?"

"Sure. We practice kung fu in gym class."

"No way."

"Yes way. There is more to kung fu than fighting, remember? Martial arts teach you how your entire body works. You learn about balance and strength, as well as flexibility and breathing. You even learn how to fall without hurting yourself, which is important for small children."

"It's important for adults, too," I said.

"True."

"So, how do we start?"

"Hmmm," she said, sizing me up. "Do *you* know how to fall?"

"Sure," I said. "I—"

Hú Dié suddenly slammed her palms into my shoulders. I stumbled backward, catching myself, but she lashed out with her bare foot and hooked my ankles. She lifted her leg into the air, and my legs went with it. I hovered momentarily above the ground like a cartoon character, then crashed onto my back. My head bounced off the mat, and I began to see stars. I lay there, staring up at the ceiling, afraid to move.

Hú Dié giggled.

I heard a door slam.

"What do you think you're doing?" Phoenix shouted. He ran over to me. "Are you okay?"

I groaned and sat up. "My ears are ringing a little, but I'll live."

"He is fine," Hú Dié said. "The floor is padded."

Phoenix turned to her and straightened. "Why did you do that?"

"He said that he knew how to fall."

"You hit him with a Double Dragon Palm Strike!"

"So? He did not fall down from it."

"True," Phoenix said. "Pretty impressive. But then you kicked his feet out with a Dragon Tail Swipe. Those are advanced moves."

"If he is ever attacked, his attacker will not select only basic moves."

"This isn't a self-defense class, you moron. Ryan just wants some exercise." Phoenix reached his hand out to me, and I grabbed it. He pulled me up effortlessly. I had no idea he was so strong.

"What would *you* teach him?" Hú Dié asked.

"Probably Tiger style," Phoenix said. "It's straight-forward and he already likes to roar."

Hú Dié shook her head. "I'm not sure. It might be too basic."

"No, it's perfect."

"I have an idea," I said. "Why don't you let *me* decide? What does Tiger style look like?"

Phoenix glared at Hú Dié. "Do you know Double Flying Tiger?"

"Of course," she said.

"Let's show him."

"Fine."

Phoenix and Hú Dié walked to the center of the room. They stopped about eight feet apart and faced one another. They calmly bowed in unison; then they suddenly sprang into the air, going for each other's throats.

I jerked backward with surprise. They'd gone from bow to blows in the blink of an eye.

Phoenix struck first. He formed a claw with his right hand and raked it toward the side of Hú Dié's neck. She tilted her head sideways, out of his reach, then thrust her own clawed hand toward Phoenix's Adam's apple.

Phoenix looked confused. He tucked his chin and turned his head, and the heel of Hú Dié's palm struck him square on the cheek. The blow sent Phoenix spinning sideways in a half twist, and he crashed to the ground. Phoenix sat up, rubbing the side of his face.

Hú Dié landed on her feet and glared down at him. "What are you doing?" she shouted. "I could have broken my hand!"

"What are *you* doing?" Phoenix countered. "You were supposed to block my blow with your forearms!"

"This is how I learned to do this form."

"I guess you learned wrong."

"Take it easy, guys," I said. "It's okay. I've seen enough."

Phoenix shook his head. "We aren't even close to being finished yet. What is the next sequence you learned, Hú Dié?"

"Tiger Catches the Kick."

"Me too. Let's see what you're made of."

Phoenix stood, and he and Hú Dié squared off again. This time they began without bowing. Hú Dié leaped high into the air and began to spin, while Phoenix only pretended to jump.

Hú Dié lashed out with one of her legs, while Phoenix

remained standing. He caught Hú Dié's spinning leg in his armpit, and he wrenched his entire body backward in a powerful arc. Hú Dié's momentum changed, and her upper body snapped like a whip. The look on her face made it clear that she hadn't been expecting this.

Phoenix dropped flat onto his back and released Hú Dié's leg, hurling her to the ground behind him. She landed on the wrestling mats with a *SLAP!* that echoed around the room.

Hú Dié staggered to her feet, and Phoenix jumped to his.

"You were supposed to jump!" Hú Dié said. "We were supposed to grab each other's kicks in the air!"

"Oh, I'm sorry," Phoenix replied. "That's not how I learned it."

"That *hurt!*" she said, rubbing her back. "You did that on purpose!"

"What was it you said when you tripped Ryan? Oh, yeah, 'The floor is padded.' You're fine."

"Leave me out of this," I said. "You two are insane. Forget about teaching me kung fu."

"No," Phoenix said. "I'm going to teach you if it's the last thing I do."

I looked him in the eye, and I could tell that he was serious.

"Can you at least teach me something that's, I don't know, less . . . violent?" I asked. "What about tai chi?"

Hú Dié snickered. "Go ahead, Phoenix. Teach him what you teach grandmothers."

"Tai chi isn't a joke," Phoenix said. "It's powerful stuff."

Hú Dié scoffed. "Sure, if you are eighty years old."

"Would you like to try it with us?" he asked.

"Okay," Hú Dié said. "I am curious to see your mastery of this most ancient art, O great *Sifu*."

Phoenix ignored her. He turned to me. "We're going to start with some basics. One of the primary foundations of tai chi is the Horse Stance. Have you ever heard of it?"

"I've seen it in movies," I said.

"Do you know why it's called that?"

"Because it looks like you're riding a horse?"

"Right."

"I don't know exactly how to do it, though."

"I'm going to show you," Phoenix said. "Begin by making fists with your hands and placing them at your sides, one on each hip. Turn your fists so that the backs are facing down and the palm sides are facing the sky. Point your elbows straight back behind you."

I did as instructed.

"Good," Phoenix said. "Now, put your feet shoulder width apart with your toes pointed forward. Keep your feet parallel with one another."

I did that, too, and Hú Dié followed along. She pretended to yawn. "Booooring," she said. "He is supposed to sweat, not fall asleep."

"Quiet," Phoenix said. "*Very* good, Ryan. Most people turn their feet out when they do that, like a duck. That's wrong. Next, bend your knees. Keep them over your feet. Don't let them bend inward or outward. At the same time, keep your head, neck, and back perfectly straight. Imagine there is a pole running from the top of your head, down through your spine, and pretend you're sitting on something low, like a stool."

It was a lot to remember, but I gave it a shot. I bent my knees until my thighs were at a forty-five-degree angle to the ground. My leg muscles began to burn a little.

"Not bad," Phoenix said. "Now try to go a little lower. Look at Hú Dié."

I glanced over to see Hú Dié with the same bored expression on her face. Her thighs were parallel to the ground.

"Seriously?" I said.

Phoenix nodded.

I groaned and sank down until I was in the same position as Hú Dié. My legs started to quiver.

"Straighten your back," Phoenix said. "Don't lean forward."

I straightened up, and nearly toppled backward. I couldn't believe how hard this was. My thighs began to scream, as well as my glutes and lower back. I felt sweat beading on my forehead.

"Good job, Ryan," Phoenix said. "Now stay in that position until lunch."

"Say what?" I said.

"Grandfather makes me stand like that for more than an hour at a time."

Hú Dié laughed. "I stand like this longer than that while I am building bikes."

"You do kung fu while you work?" I asked.

"Sure," she said. "I once stood like this for two hours while I welded bicycle frames."

I looked down at her solid legs, and I believed her.

We stood like this for a few minutes without moving. I glanced from Phoenix to Hú Dié and then back to Phoenix.

"What?" Phoenix asked.

"This is a great workout for my legs," I said, "but it really is kind of boring. Can you teach me something else while we stand here? Maybe a breathing exercise or something?"

"Fine," Phoenix said. "How about I teach you how to connect with your *chi* through breathing?"

"Cool," I said. "I could use that."

"How are your legs holding up?"

My legs were shaking noticeably from the strain of the Horse Stance, but I said, "I'm good."

Phoenix nodded. "Excellent answer. What you're going to do is breathe deeply. Instead of expanding and contracting your chest like you normally do when exercising, though, try to expand and contract just your stomach."

I tried it. It was strange but not difficult. My stomach began to warm a little on the inside.

"Do you feel anything?" Phoenix asked.

"Yeah," I said. "This may sound cheesy, but it's kind of like there's a candle burning behind my belly button."

"That's your *dan tien*. It means you're doing the technique right. Very good."

I concentrated harder, and the warming intensified. Then, like a ray of sunlight coming into sharp focus through a magnifying glass, my insides ignited. My abdominal muscles cramped tight, and my energy level dropped as if somebody had pulled a drain plug. It was the dragon bone.

I buckled forward, unable to straighten, and fell to the ground. The pain was so great, I couldn't move. I just lay there as the cramping spread from my abdomen to my chest. It continued to my neck and jaw, then down through my hips, thighs, and calves, all the way to my toes. My arms locked up at my sides, my hands contorting into arthritic claws. I'd frozen completely, as if I'd been dipped in liquid nitrogen.

"Ryan!" Phoenix said. "What's wrong?"

I couldn't answer. My vocal cords had seized up. I couldn't even open my eyes.

"Grandfather!" Phoenix shouted. "Uncle Tí! We need you! Something is happening to Ryan!"

Through the pain, I felt footsteps pounding across the wrestling mats. Uncle Tí.

"What is it?" he asked. "Did Ryan break a limb?"

"No," Phoenix said. "One minute he was doing a Horse Stance, and the next his body cramped up. He can't even talk."

"Just a Horse Stance?"

"No. I was also teaching him a basic *chi* breathing exercise with his stomach. He said that he felt a candle burning behind his belly button. Then he closed his eyes and seemed to concentrate more, and this happened."

I felt the slow, shuffling footsteps of Phoenix's grandfather approaching. "This is all my fault," he said. "The dragon bone doesn't want Ryan to control his own *chi*. How foolish of me. I should have considered this before suggesting you teach him such things."

Phoenix's grandfather was soon kneeling beside me. I

knew it was him because of his smell. His sweat smelled of dragon bone, just like mine.

"Ryan," he said, "I know you can hear me. Please forgive me. I am going to help you."

"I've never seen anything like this," Uncle Tí said. "I'll go get my medical bag. I always carry sedatives, as well as muscle relaxants."

"No," Phoenix's grandfather said. "Go to my bedroom and retrieve my acupuncture needles. Phoenix, call Ryan's mother. Tell her to come immediately."

Uncle Tí and Phoenix hurried off.

"Will he be okay?" Hú Dié asked.

"I believe so," Phoenix's grandfather replied.

"Is there anything I can do?" she asked.

"Just stay here with him as I am doing. He can hear us."

I felt Hú Dié shuffle around, like she couldn't get comfortable. "This is difficult for me," she said. "My mother has ALS—Lou Gehrig's disease. This happens to her sometimes. Like her body is rebelling against her. I hate it."

"That is unfortunate," Phoenix's grandfather said.

"It is not unfortunate; it is *unfair*. I used to want to give her dragon bone. After seeing this, I am not so sure."

Footsteps pounded against the mats again. It was both Phoenix and Uncle Tí.

"Ryan's mom is on the way," Phoenix said. "I unlocked the front door for her."

"And here is your acupuncture set," Uncle Tí said.

There was the sound of a zipper being opened, and Phoenix's grandfather said, "Give me some space."

● ● ●

I don't know how long I lay there before I opened my eyes. The pain was so great, I lost all track of time, but my mom hadn't shown up yet.

I was lying flat on my back, and the first thing I saw was Hú Dié's face. She had tears in her eyes, but she smiled at me.

I smiled back.

"Look!" Hú Dié said. "His mouth works!"

I surprised myself by laughing.

"Sounds like his vocal cords are working, too," Uncle Tí said. "Ryan, can you speak?"

"Yeah." I coughed. "My throat is really sore, though."

"Your whole body will be sore for several days," Phoenix's grandfather said. "Do not let it stop you from exercising, though. You *must* continue to fight the dragon bone."

"I will," I said. "After this experience, I wish I could just flush it from my system."

"Can you move yet?" Phoenix asked.

"I don't know," I said.

I tried to move my arms and legs, but couldn't. I did manage to lift my head, though.

My voice began to quiver. "Am I . . . paralyzed?"

"Only temporarily," Phoenix's grandfather said. "I am not finished with the procedure. You should regain the use of your limbs shortly."

I glanced down at my bare chest. More than a hundred thin needles protruded from my torso. They waved like miniature flagpoles with the rising and falling of my chest as I breathed.

I blinked. "What the—"

"Acupuncture needles," Uncle Tí said. "Grandfather is gifted in their use. Chinese have been using them for thousands of years to stimulate the flow of *chi* through various parts of a person's body. So far, it looks like what he's doing is working."

I felt my right shoulder begin to warm, and I rotated it slightly. I smiled.

Phoenix's grandfather returned the smile, but said nothing.

The door leading to the house suddenly burst open, and I saw my mother.

"Ayeeee! Stop right there! What are you doing to my boy?"

I raised my head and watched my mom struggle across the soft wrestling mats in her high heels. The fact that she was overweight didn't help. Even so, she raised her purse over her head like a warrior and rushed forward.

"No!" I said. "He's helping me. I could end up paralyzed if he messes up."

"That's right," Uncle Tí said. "Ryan is in good hands."

She ground to a halt. "Paralyzed?"

"He won't become paralyzed," Phoenix's grandfather said calmly. "I promise. What Ryan is experiencing is severe muscle cramps. The paralysis is only temporary."

My mom appeared to calm down a little. She lowered her purse. "Is that acupuncture? You endorse this medieval practice?"

"Yes, I do," Uncle Tí said. "Only we don't consider it medieval. We call it traditional Chinese medicine, or TCM.

Chinese have been doing this for thousands of years. Medieval times were six hundred years ago."

"Whatever. Couldn't you just give him some pills instead? Or maybe a shot? One needle instead of, what is that, *hundreds* of needles? My God. Doesn't that hurt, Ryan?"

"No," I said. "I actually feel better than I have in weeks."

"You look like a life-sized voodoo doll."

"Appearances can be deceiving," Phoenix's grandfather said. "One more needle, and I am finished." He looked at me. "You should rest your head back on the ground. This last one will act as a switch, connecting the remaining needles that have yet to take effect. You should feel a rush of energy, and the balance of your cramping will subside."

"Oh, dear," my mom said, "I can't watch this."

Phoenix's grandfather removed a plastic-wrapped needle from his acupuncture bag. He unwrapped the needle and tossed the plastic into a large pile of other wrappers. With steady hands, he slowly pushed the needle into the skin of my abdomen.

"I think I'm going to be sick," my mom said.

Phoenix's grandfather rotated the needle clockwise, then counterclockwise. I felt a *whoosh* of heat wash from the needle's tip outward. It was like sinking into a warm bath.

"Ahhhhh," I said. "That feels so good."

"How is the cramping?" Uncle Tí asked.

"Gone, one hundred percent."

"Can you sit up?" Phoenix's grandfather asked.

"I think so."

"Show us."

I hesitated. "What about the needles?"

"They are not going anywhere," Phoenix's grandfather said. "They need to remain in place a bit longer. You will be fine."

I pushed myself up onto my elbows; then I sat upright. Row upon row of needles shimmered up and down my torso.

My mom shuddered. "I can't believe you don't feel them. You remind me of a porcupine."

"I don't think porcupines have quills on their stomachs," I said, smiling.

"Are you dizzy?" Uncle Tí asked.

"Not at all. I haven't felt this good in a long time. Seriously." I looked at Phoenix's grandfather. "Thank you so much!"

He bowed his head slightly. "It is the least I could do. If I may make a suggestion, you should stop learning kung fu until the dragon bone bond is broken."

"*You* were learning kung fu?" my mom said. "I'm going to lock you in your room until summer vacation ends."

I sighed. "Don't be so dramatic, Mom. You can't do that. I have to exercise. Besides, children's social services will be all over you for child imprisonment."

"Fine. I'll drive you to the trail park a couple times a week. Otherwise, you'll stay locked in your room."

"Stop embarrassing me. That won't work, either. The trail is closed because of the rain. It probably won't reopen for a month."

"What are you going to do, then?" she asked.

"I don't know," I said. "I thought kung fu would be the answer."

"Can't you just wait it out? Maybe a month of rest will be good for you."

"Mrs. Vanderhausen," Uncle Tí said, "it is critical that Ryan exercise."

"I'm sorry," my mom said. "This has all been very hard on me. I should have known better than to send Ryan off to live with his uncle in the first place. My brother-in-law had a history of experimenting on people without fully disclosing possible side effects. I just never dreamed he'd do it to a child."

"Is that a fact?" Uncle Tí said. "I looked into Dr. Vanderhausen's past, but I could find nothing of the sort. No formal complaints were ever filed."

"It was all handled informally. The victims were paid off in lieu of suing him. A lot of money changed hands. How else do you think we could afford a house like ours?"

My voice caught in my throat. "You mean *Dad* was tricked by his own brother? Is that how he got cancer?"

"No," my mom replied. "I was."

"Huh?"

"Your weight," Uncle Tí said.

My mother nodded. "I was part of Dr. V's very first diet drug trial. The concoction he gave me ruined my pituitary gland. No matter how little I eat, I continue to slowly gain weight. I've been meaning to tell you for years, Ryan. I suppose I've been too embarrassed at my own stupidity for trusting him."

"Oh, man," I said, "I had no idea. That stinks!"

My mom took my hand. "Let's not dwell on the past. We need to figure out how to deal with the present. You have to exercise, but the trail is closed. Can you ride somewhere else?"

"*All* the mountain bike trails will be affected by the rain, Mrs. Vanderhausen," Phoenix said.

"Well, do you have to ride a mountain bike, Ryan?" she asked. "What about a cyclocross bike?"

"A cyclocross course would stay open for a day or even a weekend in heavy rain," I said, "but not any longer. The ground would get too torn up."

"How about riding a road bike? Like your father?"

I frowned. "I don't know. Those tires are awful skinny for someone as big as me, especially on wet pavement."

"Ryan," Hú Dié said, "your mom might be onto something. Road bikes handle pretty well in the rain. Have you ever ridden one?"

"Not since I tried my dad's when I was little."

"You would not have noticed, then, that they are actually quite rugged. I know you've watched the Tour de France. Those riders torture their bikes."

Phoenix chuckled. *"Rugged? Torture?* As soon as those guys get a speck of dirt on their bike, they swap it out for a new one from their crew following behind in a support vehicle."

"It is not like that at all," Hú Dié said. "You should consider giving road biking a try, Ryan."

I shook my head. "Maybe if the weather was better. And I had a coach. I've seen stages of some of the cycling tours on TV and the Internet. Road riding is a lot more involved than mountain biking or cyclocross."

"That's what makes it more interesting," Hú Dié said.

"No, that is what makes it *less* interesting," Phoenix countered. "It's too much work."

Hú Dié looked at me. "See, I told you he was lazy."

"What do you mean by that?" Phoenix asked.

"Nothing," Hú Dié said.

I glanced at my mom. She hadn't said a word. That wasn't like her at all.

"What are you thinking, Mom?" I asked.

"My cousin in California," she said.

I grinned.

"You mean the one who . . . you know?" Phoenix asked awkwardly.

She frowned. "Yes, Peter, the one who used to race with Ryan's father. The one who went on to race at an elite level and coach other riders. Maybe Ryan could spend a little time with him."

"It sounds great, but do you think he'd do it?" I asked.

"In a heartbeat," she said. "He adores you. I think you remind him of himself when he was young."

"He is awesome," I said. "His arms look like anacondas."

"Let me make a phone call," she said. "Excuse me." She began to totter toward the door.

"Take your shoes off, Mom. It will be easier to walk on the mats."

She laughed. "Oh, right. Thanks."

After she had gone, Hú Dié said, "The more I see of your mom, the more I like her."

"She can be a little embarrassing," I said, "but I couldn't ask for a better mom. I had no idea about her . . . um . . . condition."

"It happens," Uncle Tí said.

"Your mother cares deeply about you," Phoenix's grandfather said. "Now lie back down. Those needles have been in you long enough."

I lay down, and Phoenix's grandfather quickly removed the needles. His hands were fast and steady, the complete opposite of the shakiness I'd seen in him earlier. He must have noticed me watching because he leaned forward and whispered in my ear. "I had a small amount of dragon bone in my acupuncture bag. I took it to steady myself in order to do this properly. I will go back to my previous half dosages tomorrow. I do *not* condone this behavior. Understand?"

"Yes, sir," I said.

He nodded. A minute later, he was done. "See if you can stand," he said.

I stood without any problems.

"Dizzy?" Uncle Tí asked.

"Nope," I said. "I feel great."

"And look at your side."

I twisted around and examined my left side. There was no sign of any previous injury. Even the scrapes were gone. I shook my head.

My mother entered from the house. "Ryan! Good news! How would you, Phoenix, and Hú Dié *all* like to go to California for ten days?"

Hú Dié's eyes lit up. "California! Sure! To ride?"

"Yes," my mom said. "Peter said that Ryan would learn

better with additional riders. We'll even invite Jake. The more, the merrier, according to Peter. He'll be able to free up his schedule. How do you feel about that, Ryan?"

"It sounds like a riot!" I said. "Did you ask what the weather is going to be like?"

"As always in July, dry as a bone."

"Where exactly does he live?" Hú Dié asked.

"Carmel. Or technically, Carmel-by-the-Sea. Funny, isn't it? We live in Carmel, Indiana, and he lives in Carmel, California. We pronounce it like the candy, though, and they don't. I guess we're sweeter than they are." She grinned.

Phoenix hadn't said a word.

"What about you, Phoenix?" my mom asked. "Don't you want to go, too?"

"I don't know," he said. "I don't have a road bike."

"Ryan doesn't, either," my mom said. "I plan to buy road bikes for all of you! Jake, too, if he wants to go. You'd be doing Ryan a tremendous favor. Paying for your expenses is the least I could do."

"The flights and everything?" Phoenix asked.

"Of course."

Phoenix shook his head. "I can't accept all that from you."

My mom turned to Phoenix's grandfather. "The money would come from my settlement with my brother-in-law. In a way, it's like he's financing the trip. I should tell you, though, that I won't be able to go. I have to finalize a few things with his estate. But the kids will be in safe hands with my cousin. He's a great guy. In fact, I met my husband through him."

"I will allow Phoenix to go," he replied, "but the decision is his to make."

"Please come, Phoenix," Hú Dié said. "We need a sprinter. You would be the one we would set up to win a race."

"I'm not sure . . . ," Phoenix said. "What do you think, Ryan?"

"I think it will be awesome," I said with a grin. "The more, the merrier. For real."

"Okay, then," Phoenix said. "When do we go?"

"Wonderful!" my mother said. She looked at Uncle Tí. "Peter said that he's busy for the next three days, but he could work with the kids for ten days after that. Do you think Ryan will be okay to ride by then?"

"I believe he's fine right now," Uncle Tí said. He turned to Phoenix's grandfather. "What do you think?"

"He seems good as new," Phoenix's grandfather said. "Perhaps better than new. I would be surprised if he has another episode like this. He would benefit greatly from the bicycle training. I believe he should go."

"What about my dragon bone amounts?" I asked.

"I'll figure it out and we'll mail the ten days' worth to your cousin," Uncle Tí said. "I'd rather you didn't try to take it onto an airplane."

"Maybe we can ship it with the gear," my mom suggested. "Peter said that I should buy the bikes and other gear here and have it sent to him. It's going to cost more, but it will save a lot of time, and I want Ryan to spend as much time on the bike as possible out there. Phoenix, Hú Dié— are you available tomorrow?"

"Sure," Hú Dié said.

"Me too," Phoenix said.

"Perfect!" my mom said. "Ryan, you should call Jake right now. If he can go on the trip, ask him if he can join us tomorrow. We're going shopping!"

"This is going to be so rad!" Jake said as we all entered Nebo Ridge Bike Shop the next morning. His folks said that he could go to California, and he seemed to be more excited than any of us, which was saying a lot.

Tim, the owner, walked over with an espresso cup in his hand. He smiled warmly. "Well, well! If it isn't the Vanderhausens and company. Welcome, Susan, Ryan, Phoenix, Jake, and . . ."

"Hú Dié," Hú Dié said. She stuck out her hand. "Pleased to meet you, sir."

Tim shook her hand. "The pleasure is all mine, Ms. Hoo-DEE-ay. I'm Tim."

She grinned. "You are the second person I have met in Indiana who can say my name properly."

"I lived overseas for a time," Tim replied. "Occupational perk of international law. Now I mostly just hang out here."

Hú Dié glanced around. "Nice place to hang out."

"Hú Dié and her father own a bike shop in China," I said.

"Really?" Tim said. "Excellent. Take a look around. Let me know if you see anything I can improve."

"Okay," Hú Dié said, "but it all looks great so far. What is that room off to the side, a training space?"

"Exactly. We offer off-season training classes for our customers, as well as for our race team members. During the racing season, we ride outside twice a week. We hold the largest weekly rides in the country. Some days, more than two hundred fifty people show up."

"That is amazing," Hú Dié said.

"Join us sometime."

"I would love to. We have come here to look at road bikes."

"You've come to the right place," Tim said. "Let me know if there's anything I can do for you—all of you."

"Thanks," we said.

Tim nodded. "Susan, can I get you an espresso? Cappuccino? On the house."

"No coffee, thank you," my mom said, "but we're going to take lots of your time. I need to outfit all four of these rascals. I'm sending them off to train for ten days with my cousin in California."

"Peter?" Tim asked.

"That's the one," my mom said. "If we find what we need today, how quickly can you get four bikes to Carmel-by-the-Sea?"

"Well, there is an airport in Monterey. We could put

everything on a plane and get it there tomorrow. Someone would have to pick it up at the airport, though. If you could wait two days, we could probably get it right to Peter's door."

"Two days would be perfect."

"Let me see what I can do." Tim headed into a small office. Looking around, I saw a guy I didn't recognize working alone in the maintenance area. He nodded at me. I nodded back.

"What are you guys waiting for?" my mom asked. "Get to it!"

We spread out, going to the racks of road bikes first. I had no idea where to start, so I just looked for the one with the coolest paint job. I grabbed a bike and began to pull it off the rack.

"Not that one," Hú Dié said, walking over to me.

"Why not?" I asked.

"The frame is too small. You need one that is fifty-seven centimeters high. That one is fifty-six."

"Where do you see the label?"

"No label. Trust me. It is a fifty-six and you need a fifty-seven."

"What difference does a centimeter make on top tube height?"

Hú Dié groaned. "You do not know anything about road bikes, do you?"

"No."

"Then go pick out some shoes or something and leave the bike to me."

"Hú Dié," my mom said, "perhaps you should pick out everybody's bikes."

"Sure," Hú Dié replied. "Hey, guys! Pick out shoes, helmets, bibs, jerseys, socks, gloves, and glasses—try to get clothes that match. It will make us look cool. I am going to take care of the bikes."

"Ah, man," Jake said. "I want to pick mine."

"Then come over here," Hú Dié said. "I will help you."

Jake ran over to Hú Dié, and I walked over to Phoenix. He was staring at a rack of mountain bikes.

"Are you fine with this?" I asked.

"Sure," he said.

"You don't mind Hú Dié picking out your bike?"

"It's not my bike, Ryan. It's your mom's. I'm going to give it back when we're done."

I sighed. "Don't be that way, Phoenix."

"What way? I appreciate what your mom is doing, but I know Hú Dié. She's going to pick good ones. I just don't feel right hanging on to a bike that costs thousands of dollars. If it makes you feel better, I'll keep the new helmet and other gear, though I don't know why we need to get new stuff. We all have gear already."

"It's different gear, especially the shoes. Roadies have their own style and their own ways of doing things."

"I'm not a roadie."

"You will be for ten days."

"Whatever. I'm *not* shaving my legs, though."

I glanced at the peach fuzz on Phoenix's knees, poking out beneath his cargo shorts. "Shave what?"

Phoenix rolled his eyes.

"Hey, guys!" Jake called out from across the shop. "Check me out!"

THE FIVE ANCESTORS OUT OF THE ASHES

I turned and saw him straddling a killer bike. It had a carbon frame and carbon rims.

Phoenix lowered his voice. "That rig has got to be at least five grand. Maybe ten. I'm telling you now, I won't ride one of those."

"Suit yourself," I said. "I think it's sweet."

I headed for Jake and shouted, "Hey, bro, where can I get one of those sick rides?"

Before long, the four of us were all geared up and sitting atop our new bikes in the back of the shop. Hú Dié, Jake, and I had high-end models, while Phoenix's was a solid entry-level road bike. Hú Dié had convinced Tim to let her have free rein of his maintenance area, and she'd adjusted each of our bikes in record time. Tim was so impressed, he offered her a job on the spot. She declined, to the relief of the new guy.

"Nice choice of bikes," Tim said as he looked us over one last time. "Great outfits, too. You really look like a team."

Hú Dié beamed.

"I agree," I said. "Can we take them for a spin?"

"Sure," Tim said. "The rain isn't too bad at the moment, but don't go too far, especially if you haven't ridden on the road much. It's a lot different from a mountain bike trail."

"I ride through the city in China every day," Hú Dié said. "I can give them some pointers."

"Even so," Tim said, "it's better to be safe than sorry."

"We understand," I said. "Where should we go?"

"I suggest our five-mile loop."

"Five miles!" Jake said. "I thought you said we shouldn't go too far."

"Five miles is nothing on a road bike if you're working hard," Hú Dié said. "That is less than ten minutes on a sunny day with no traffic."

Jake's eyes widened. "That's like . . . let me see . . . thirty miles an hour!"

"Yes," Hú Dié said. "That is on flat ground. Roadies can easily go faster, especially on downhill runs. They can hit one hundred kilometers per hour on steep downhills, which is more than sixty miles per hour."

"All right!" Jake exclaimed.

"Don't get your hopes up," Tim said. "You'll be going slower than thirty miles per hour today. The rain may have lessened, but it's still a little treacherous. Be careful out there. Don't do anything stupid." He looked at my mom. "Would you like me to ride with them, Susan?"

"Heavens, no," my mom said. "But thank you for the offer. I'll follow behind in my car like I used to for my husband and cousin when they raced together. I know how to keep a safe distance."

"Perfect," Tim said. "I'd feel better if someone kept an eye on them."

My mom turned to us. "What do you say, kids? Are you ready to hit the road?"

Hú Dié, Jake, and I said, "Yeah!"

Phoenix said nothing.

Tim showed us a map and pointed out the easy-to-remember route.

"I'm going to get the car out front," my mom said. "Don't start until you see me pull around the building behind you.

Pay no attention to me as you're riding. It's my job to keep an eye on all of you, not the other way around."

She left, and we pushed our bikes through the back door into the slow, steady rain. This shower was gentle compared to yesterday's downpour, but today's was cooler. I felt a shiver run down my spine as we lined up in the parking lot.

My mom pulled around the building and lined up behind us. She tapped the horn.

"That's our cue," I said.

"I will take the lead," Hú Dié said.

"No, I'll do it," I said.

Hú Dié shrugged. "If you wish. Are we going to race?"

"No," I said. "This is just a friendly ride."

We rolled through the parking lot single file. Hú Dié was behind me, followed by Phoenix. Jake was riding caboose.

Within two revolutions of my pedals, I remembered how much I enjoyed the few times I'd been on a road bike. It just felt so . . . solid. Mountain bikes had shock absorbers, which were great for smoothing out trail bumps, but they also absorbed a fair amount of pedaling energy. Road bikes were far more efficient because they were rigid. Jake had almost had a heart attack when he saw Hú Dié pump his road bike tires up to one hundred fifteen pounds per square inch. Mountain bike tires were usually run at thirty-five or forty pounds.

I turned out of the parking lot, onto the main road. It was an amazing feeling leading the pack. I could see everything. On a mountain bike trail, most of the time all you see is a blur of trees. Out here, the light rain felt good on my face, and I enjoyed the wind against my shoulders as I rode. The bottoms of my feet were connected to the tops of my pedals, just like on my mountain and cyclocross bikes, only here I was able to keep my pedal stroke uniform and ride at a consistent speed because there weren't any obstacles to screw up my cadence. My legs never felt so good.

Hú Dié had installed bike computers on our handlebars, and I glanced down at my display.

Fifteen miles per hour.

I looked back and saw that my mother was about a quarter mile behind us. She seemed to be going the same speed we were traveling. Headlights flashed behind her, and a vehicle pulled around, passing her and quickly picking up speed.

"Car!" Jake shouted, and before I could react, the little sports car was rushing alongside us. It hit a long puddle in the road as it passed and threw up a huge wake, washing filthy water over all of us. Bits of grit clung to the tip of my nose and lips. I spat.

"Slow down, jerk!" Jake yelled, even though the car was already long gone.

I blinked several times, wishing I'd worn my sleek new riding sunglasses to keep water from splashing into my eyes.

"Here comes another!" Jake shouted. "And it's a big one!"

I slowed and veered over to the rightmost edge of the road, crossing the painted lane boundary and hugging the fringe of the asphalt that dropped four inches to a wide gravel shoulder. With my mountain or 'cross bike, I would have hopped down there in a second. However, I knew I'd be toast with the skinny tires of this road bike, so I kept my line, hugged the fringe, and gripped my handlebars tight as the next vehicle approached.

It was a large SUV, and it passed so close that I could have licked the passenger side mirror. The vehicle's pressure wave pushed against me, threatening to knock me over the drop. Fortunately, I was able to hold my line until the SUV cleared me and continued up the road.

"Idiot!" Jake shouted. "There was no reason for you to drive that close to us! You had the whole road!"

I glanced back at Hú Dié. "This kind of sucks," I said.

"This is nothing," Hú Dié said. "You should see Kaifeng. Just ask Phoenix. It will be better once we are off of this main road."

We made it to our turnoff without any additional vehicles passing us. The new road was a residential street, and no one was out. I decided to stretch my legs a bit, and I picked up speed. I was beginning to enjoy myself again. Most of the grit had washed off my face, and I no longer held my handlebars in a death grip.

"Now we're talking!" Jake said from the back. "Lead us to the Promised Land, Beefcake!"

Hú Dié groaned. "Is he always like this?"

"Pretty much," I said.

I glanced down at my bike's display unit.

Twenty miles per hour.

I wasn't even pedaling that hard.

"Push it some more!" Hú Dié shouted.

I began to hammer. The speed on my display began to rise.

Twenty-two miles per hour.

Twenty-four.

Twenty-six.

"Whoo-hoo!" Jake shouted.

"How are you doing up there, Ryan?" Hú Dié called. "You want me to pull for a bit?"

"Huh?" I shouted over my shoulder.

"Pull," she repeated. "Do you want to draft off of me like I have been drafting off of you?"

"No!" I shouted. "I like it up here. I've got plenty left in my tank."

"Go, Ryan!"

"Is that all you've got, *Beefcake*?" someone shouted, and I realized it was Phoenix. I glanced behind me to see him veer out of the line and begin to catch up to Hú Dié.

"Oh, no, you don't!" she shouted. She tried to veer out of the line, but Phoenix sprinted alongside her, cutting off her exit.

"Going somewhere?" he asked. I saw that his eyes were flashing with green fire.

Hú Dié scowled. "This is dangerous, Phoenix. Get back in line."

"How about I make my own line?" he shouted, and he shot forward, passing me.

"I don't think so!" Hú Dié growled, and she shot past me, too.

I looked down at my display. Twenty-eight miles per hour.

We rounded a turn, and Jake pulled up behind my rear wheel, drafting. "Holy cow!" he shouted. "Those two are nuts!"

"You know it!" I shouted back.

"Let's get 'em!" Jake said.

"All right!"

"You want me to pull?" Jake asked.

"No—I'm enjoying this."

"Bonus!" Jake cried.

I shifted gears and let my legs rip as we rounded another turn.

From what I remembered of the map, we were probably halfway back to the shop. I looked over my shoulder at my mother and saw that she was now much closer behind us, driving the same speed we were riding. She didn't look happy.

I glanced at my display again.

Thirty miles per hour.

"Yee-haw!" Jake shouted. "Giddy up, cowboy!"

I continued to hammer. I could see Phoenix in the distance with Hú Dié drafting off of his back tire. I once read that the person drafting expends as much as 30 percent less energy than the person pulling in front.

"Look!" Jake shouted. "They're slowing down."

When I'd raced a cyclocross bike against Phoenix in Texas, he'd sprinted by me, but I soon passed him again. He could ride faster than the wind, but only for a short distance. Me, I could keep a faster-than-average pace all day.

"Is that the shop?" Jake asked.

"Where?" I shouted.

"Ahead of Phoenix and Hú Dié. It's a little difficult to see with the rain, but I'm pretty sure that's it. Let's show them how to finish a race. Take me home, my man!"

"Roger that," I yelled, and I sprinted with all I had.

My mom honked her horn.

"She wants us to slow down!" Jake shouted.

I glanced at my display.

Thirty-five miles per hour.

"Don't worry about my mom!" I shouted. "Just focus on catching Phoenix and Hú Dié."

"Got it!"

Phoenix and Hú Dié were now only fifty feet ahead of us, and I was closing the gap fast. Hú Dié glanced over her shoulder and flashed a brilliant smile, then rocketed around Phoenix.

"Look at her go!" Jake shouted. "Yeah, baby!"

Jake and I blew past Phoenix, too, and I saw the fire go out in his eyes.

We were only a few hundred yards from the shop now, and Hú Dié was beginning to slow. Even so, I knew I could never catch her. Jake, however, had been conserving energy by drafting off of me.

"Thanks for the lift, bro!" Jake shouted, and he blew past me.

I glanced down at my display.

Thirty-eight miles per hour.

I changed gears and began to slow, but I still kept my legs moving. I knew that cooling down after a ride was important. I looked back at Phoenix and saw that he wasn't even pedaling anymore. He'd given up. My mom pulled alongside him and they exchanged a few words.

Ahead, Jake was about to catch Hú Dié. I watched in amazement as the goof-off kid who always came in second or third place in our mountain bike races passed Hú Dié, crossing into the shop parking lot an entire bike length ahead of her.

I heard Hú Dié's and Jake's brakes squeal as they slowed and stopped. I reached them as Hú Dié was bumping fists with Jake.

"Ouch!" Jake said, sucking wind. "What do you have inside your riding glove? Steel?"

Hú Dié giggled as she, too, struggled to catch her breath. "Just my fist. Congratulations!"

Jake was all smiles. "Thanks!" he huffed. "I couldn't have done it without Ryan, though."

"Yes," Hú Dié said, "drafting off of him is like drafting behind a semitrailer. It is awesome."

I smiled, breathing hard. "My pleasure."

My mom pulled up in her car and parked beside us. She jumped out of the vehicle, into the rain. "What is *wrong* with you kids? Are you trying to kill yourselves?"

"Ah—" I began say.

"Save it," she barked. "If I hadn't already bought the plane tickets to California and your gear, I would cancel the entire trip!"

"I'm sorry," I huffed.

"Me too," huffed Jake.

"And me," huffed Hú Dié.

My mom took several deep breaths herself and sighed. "Promise you won't do something stupid like that again. I've seen firsthand what a bike wreck can do to a person, especially in the rain. I don't want anything to happen to any of you."

"Promise," the three of us huffed.

"Thank you," she said.

Phoenix coasted over to us, but he kept his eyes lowered. Rainwater trickled through the deep frown lines in his cheeks.

"What's wrong, bro?" Jake asked.

"Nothing," Phoenix said. "I just hate to lose."

"That was not a race," Hú Dié said. "It was a mistake. We should not have done that in the first place."

"Whatever," Phoenix said. "Road biking isn't my thing. Maybe I shouldn't go to California."

"Oh, no, mister," my mom said. "You agreed to go, and you are going to keep your word! Besides, you're the team's sprinter. Somebody has to cross the finish line first."

"I'll do it!" Jake joked.

Phoenix cocked his head toward Jake. His eyes narrowed slightly, and I saw a flash of green fire in them. "Is that a challenge?"

"Maybe," Jake replied.

"That's settles it," Phoenix said. "I'll see you in Cali."

"Bring it, bro!" Jake said.

STAGE TWO

ATTACK:

A sudden attempt to get away
from another rider

"Ryan! Over here!"

I looked across the terminal at the Monterey, California, airport and saw Peter cruising toward us, riding low to the ground. He'd gotten a new wheelchair.

I waved back. "Yo! Peter! Great to see you, man!"

I turned to Phoenix, Jake, and Hú Dié. Phoenix and Jake knew about Peter's accident, but Hú Dié stood with her mouth agape.

"I guess I forgot to mention that my cousin's in a wheelchair," I said. "He was in a bad bike crash years ago and broke his back."

Hú Dié's eyes widened. "Your cousin is Peter *Hathaway*?"

"Yeah," I said. "That's my mother's maiden name—Hathaway. You've heard of him?"

"Of course! I have seen him in several different cycling magazines. Who could forget arms like *those*? He is a hand-cycling pioneer!"

Peter rolled up, and I noticed that his short brown hair was now a little gray at the temples, but otherwise he looked the same. His thick shoulders and gigantic arms looked like they might split his t-shirt any moment. We both smiled, and I gave him a bro hug.

"You've really filled out," Peter said.

"I hit the gym when I can," I replied.

"We need to talk about that. Introductions first?"

I turned to Hú Dié. She was blushing. "Peter, this is Hú Dié. She's visiting from China."

Hú Dié stepped forward and stuck out her hand. "A pleasure to meet you."

"A pleasure to meet you, too," Peter said, and he took her hand. "Hey! You have a strong grip!"

Hú Dié let go of his hand. "Sorry," she said, looking embarrassed.

Peter laughed. "No need to be sorry. I'm impressed!"

"Um, thank you," Hú Dié said.

Jake extended his hand and stepped up beside Hú Dié. "Hi, I'm Jake."

"Nice to meet you, Jake," Peter said, taking Jake's hand. Peter's hand completely engulfed Jake's. "Ryan's mother has told me a lot about you."

"Uh-oh," Jake said.

Peter smiled. "I meant that as a compliment. She's actually told me a lot about all of you." He turned to Phoenix. "Especially you. Phoenix, I presume."

Phoenix shook Peter's hand. "Nice to finally meet you, sir."

"Call me Peter or Coach," Peter said, "anything but *sir.* It makes me feel old."

"Yes, sir," Phoenix said. "I mean, Coach."

"That's better," Peter said. "I hear you're our sprinter, Phoenix."

Jake scoffed good-naturedly.

Peter looked at him, then back at Phoenix. "Do I detect a little friendly competition?"

Phoenix shrugged.

"There is no competition," Jake said. *"I'm* the man." He laughed.

"Sounds like a rivalry to me," Peter said. "That's healthy among teammates. However, you must agree to respect my decisions. I will select roles for each of you, and you will perform those roles. Road racing is a team sport."

"Of course," Jake said. "I'm just messing with Phoenix. I'll do whatever you tell me to do."

"Me too," Phoenix said.

"And me," Hú Dié said.

"Likewise," I said.

"Perfect," Peter said. "Let's get out of here."

We headed for baggage claim, and Peter turned to me. "About your physique, Ryan. You might want to lay off the upper-body workouts. You're not planning to race hand-cycles, too, are you?"

"No," I replied.

"Then all that mass you're carrying upstairs is just extra weight. We'll see if we can come up with a program to help you tone it down."

"No way!" Hú Dié said.

We all turned to her, and she blushed.

"Er," she said, "what I mean is, the wider Ryan is, the better we can draft off of him. He pulls like an ox."

Peter looked surprised. "Is that so? I always figured you were more of a sprinter, Ryan. You seemed to like the limelight."

"I don't know," I said. "I think I might like pulling better."

"I can't say I blame you," Peter said. "Pulling was my favorite, too. I enjoyed dictating the pace, and the scenery is much better up front. You can see the entire countryside when you're leading the pack, whereas in the middle of the peloton you mostly see the back of some other guy's bike. Did you know that I used to pull for your dad?"

"I just found that out. My mom showed me some old pictures last night."

"They're not *that* old," Peter said with a laugh.

"Sixteen years," I said. "I wasn't even born yet."

"Well, to you, they're old. To me, it seems like yesterday."

We arrived at the baggage carousel and grabbed our things. The airport was tiny, and two minutes later we were outside in the comfortable afternoon breeze. It was twenty degrees cooler than the ninety-degree temperatures we always had in Indiana in July. Unlike the flat terrain of central Indiana, the land here was very hilly, making for a nice change in scenery, too.

"Perfect temperature," Jake said. "Awesome views. Why would anybody live in the Midwest?"

"Beats me," Peter said.

In the parking lot, Peter wheeled up to an old minivan that I remembered from my last visit. "Load your bags into the back and climb in," he said. "Take any seat you'd like except the passenger seat."

As I stacked our luggage behind the rear bench seat, Jake leaned over to me and whispered, "*Peter* is going to drive this thing?"

"Sure," I said. "It has special hand controls."

"Where is the ramp for him to get inside?"

"He doesn't need one. Watch."

I closed the rear door as Peter opened the driver's door. He positioned his chair next to the driver's seat, locked the chair's brakes, and hauled first his torso and then his legs into the van. Next, he bent down and unlocked the chair's brakes and removed the quick-release wheels, pulling the wheels into the van and setting them on the floor in front of the passenger seat. He removed the seat cushion from his wheelchair and folded the chair up like an accordion. Then he cranked the driver's seat all the way back and pulled the cushion and chair over himself, setting both on the passenger seat. Finally, he cranked his seat back up and closed the door.

"That was cool," Jake said as we climbed into the back of the van.

"It sure was," Hú Dié said. "Those wheels look a lot like bike rims."

"They are," Peter replied. "Even the tires are similar, except most chair tires still use inner tubes. Bike tires usually run tubeless these days."

"What are these tracks on the floor?" Jake asked as he closed the door.

"Those are for my friends to tie down their wheelchairs and connect seat belt extensions," Peter said. "I rarely use the bench seats. I have a makeshift ramp that I haul around, and it's easiest for my friends to just stay in their chairs. Someday I might spring for a power lift, but we're all in decent shape and enjoy making do with as little specialized equipment as possible."

I thought about when I was temporarily paralyzed by dragon bone. I couldn't imagine what it must be like to be in Peter's shoes, or his friends'.

"You are very inspiring," Hú Dié said.

"Just living life," Peter said.

He started the engine and pulled out of the parking lot, using a lever mounted on the steering wheel column to control both the gas and brakes. Riding with him didn't feel any different from riding with my mother.

"I live quite close to the airport," Peter said. "We should be there in less than twenty minutes. Do you guys have any questions?"

Jake cleared his throat. "I do, but you don't have to answer it if you don't want to."

"You're wondering what happened to my legs."

"Yeah."

"I don't mind talking about it," Peter said. "I was road racing in the rain. I was at the head of the peloton, and I'd just *fallen off*—that is, I moved off to the side to allow one of my teammates to take the lead—when he hit a pothole. He went down, along with me and twenty other guys. I think we were doing close to thirty miles per hour at the time. Several guys suffered broken limbs, and I broke my back."

"Whoa," Jake said. "When was that?"

"Sixteen years ago. I don't remember much about it; one minute, I was swerving to avoid my teammate, and the next I was in a hospital unable to move my legs."

"I'm so sorry," Hú Dié said.

"Don't be," Peter replied. "It was just one of those things. People die in races every year, even pros on the big tours. I won't say that I was lucky, but I will say that I was fortunate. Although things might have ended up differently if my teammate would have simply shouted 'hole' before he hit it. This is why it's so important to learn to communicate while riding, especially if you plan on drafting. Safety needs to come first. Competition is second." He paused. "Ryan's mother told me that you guys were drafting a couple days ago, in the rain, no less. If I see any one of you doing that before I teach you how to do it properly, I'll send you *all* home. Got it?"

"Got it," we all said.

"Good," Peter said. "Now that that is out of the way, let's talk about something more fun—your bikes. They arrived earlier today. They're in my garage."

"How many boxes?" Hú Dié asked.

"Three. I didn't open them, but based on the size, one looks like bike frames, one is probably wheels, and the last one is gear."

"Three is the magic number," Hú Dié said. "I packed the boxes myself."

I couldn't wait to open the boxes. Uncle Tí had given Hú Dié a tiny vial of dragon bone to include in the shipment, and she'd stuffed it into my bike's hollow seat post. It wasn't the greatest hiding place, but it was better than my trying to sneak the dragon bone onto our airplane.

"Oh, my," Hú Dié said suddenly.

"Sweet!" Jake said.

I glanced out the window and grinned. The strip malls and residential neighborhoods we'd been driving past disappeared, replaced by meadows of rolling hills. A canopy of trees covered the road. We drove over a stone bridge, and I caught a glimpse of the sea down a steep slope to our right. It looked like something out of a fairy tale.

"Nice scenery," Phoenix said, "but where are we supposed to ride? This road is pretty narrow, and we're right on the edge of a cliff."

"That's a surprise I'm saving for tomorrow morning," Peter said. "It's not far, and it's quite safe. If you like it here, you'll love it there."

We slowed and turned onto a side road, bouncing along pockmarked asphalt that rose and fell between towering eucalyptus trees. Peter lowered his window, and I could hear and smell the ocean. We drove around a sharp bend, and surf crashed against rocks just a few feet from the pavement. The only thing separating us from the sea foam was a knee-high stone railing. The other side of the narrow road didn't have a shoulder, either, just a tall hill of solid rock.

"I am speechless," Hú Dié said.

"I'm not!" Jake said. "This is the coolest! Wow!"

"I'm glad you like it," Peter said. "I have a small place just up this next hill."

The van climbed the steep slope, and we pulled into

Peter's driveway. He hit the button on his garage door opener, and the door began to rise.

"Look at that!" Hú Dié exclaimed. "I might never go into the house!"

Peter had converted his garage into a small machine shop where he built custom handcycles for himself and others. Tools and machines were neatly arranged atop a series of low workbenches. Cycles in different stages of completion hung from winches attached to the ceiling.

Peter turned to Hú Dié. "You like to look at mechanical things?"

Phoenix laughed. "She likes to *build* mechanical things. She has the craziest bike I've ever seen. She even named it: *Trixie.*"

"Really?" Peter said. "Ryan's mother told me that you and your father owned a bike shop, but she didn't mention that your employees actually build them."

Hú Dié flashed her brilliant smile. "*I* build them."

"You assemble everything yourself?" Peter asked.

"Yes. I fabricate the frames, too. We have tube benders and a TIG welder. I even paint the frames."

"You bend steel?"

"Sometimes," Hú Dié said. "Most of our customers want aluminum, though. It is so much lighter."

"It sure is," Peter said. "Do you know how to weld aluminum?"

"Sure. It took a few years to get the hang of it. Now I weld aluminum for other people, too. Not a lot of people know how to do it."

"I got that," Peter said. "I've been trying for years, but I still keep blowing holes in my frames. I end up spending a fortune to have my bikes welded by someone else, and a lot of times *they* don't even get it right."

"I can teach you how to do it," Hú Dié offered.

"Really?"

She nodded. "Although it is going to cost you."

"Oh?"

"I want to ride one of your handcycles."

"Is that all?" Peter said. "Come on, then. You can try one right now! I want to close this deal before you change your mind."

8

We unloaded our luggage; then Phoenix, Jake, Peter, and I waited inside the garage while Hú Dié disappeared into the house. She soon reappeared wearing our new "team" cycling jersey and padded riding bib shorts, as well as new white socks and racing shoes. She pulled her long black hair into a ponytail and shook out her legs, stretching them. Her thighs rippled like the shoulders of a powerful feline.

"You know you won't be using your legs at all with this handcycle, right?" Peter asked.

"Yes," Hú Dié said. "I just feel a little stiff after the plane ride."

I rolled my eyes. She wanted to show off her muscles to Peter.

Peter pointed to two cycles he'd lowered from the ceiling. Both were hand-powered trikes with three wheels, but one was low to the ground with two wheels in back and one in front, while the other was higher and had one wheel in back and two in front. The higher one also had knobby off-road tires and a seat that appeared to have long armrests.

"Which one would you like to try?" Peter asked.

"Both!" Hú Dié said.

Peter laughed. "All right, but you can only ride one at a time."

"I'll ride the other one," Jake said.

"Not before I get a chance," I said. "He's *my* cousin."

"You can all have a turn," Peter said. "Let's get Hú Dié squared away first."

"Thank you," Hú Dié said, eyeing both bikes. "One is for off-road, and the other is for riding on pavement, yes?"

"That's right," Peter said. "The low one with the single wheel in front is a road cycle. You sit in it like a regular chair. The higher one is a mountain cycle. See those things that look like armrests on the mountain cycle? They're actually for your legs. You kneel on them. There is also a pad to rest your chest against."

"I will try the mountain handcycle first," Hú Dié said. "I like road riding, but I enjoy mountain biking more."

"Sounds good. The mountain cycle is better suited for the crumbling asphalt of my neighborhood streets, anyway. I can't wait for them to be resurfaced."

Hú Dié climbed onto the mountain cycle, and Peter strapped her in, binding her ankles and bent legs to the cycle's frame. If she crashed, she'd stay attached to the bike.

"You'll notice the hand crank arms on this cycle are set a hundred eighty degrees apart, like on a regular bicycle," Peter said. "Your arms will work in opposition, just like your legs work in opposition on a regular bike. You can lift yourself to absorb bumps by straightening your elbows slightly, just like you'd rise up out of your saddle on a regular bike by straightening your knees a little."

Hú Dié glanced at the road handcycle. "Those hand cranks are different."

"That's right," Peter said. "The cranks on that cycle are parallel with one another. Your arms go around in unison. Parallel cranks help you go faster over flat ground because you can really get your torso behind each revolution. However, cranks set a hundred eighty degrees apart are better for climbing because you're providing continuous power. There aren't any dead spots in your stroke."

"Makes sense," Hú Dié said. "Where are the brakes, and how do you steer this thing?"

"Both types of cycles have brake levers and gear shifters mounted to the hand cranks. To steer the road cycle, you turn the hand cranks like a steering wheel. On this mountain cycle, the chest support does the steering. You simply lean in the direction you want to go, kind of like riding a motorcycle."

"I understand," Hú Dié said.

"Ryan," Peter said, "see if you can find the helmets in the smallest of those three boxes that came from Indiana."

I opened the box and tossed Hú Dié her helmet. She strapped it on.

"Be careful," Peter told her. "Trikes seem like they'd be more stable than a two-wheeled cycle, but they aren't. If you lean too far the wrong way into a turn, you're going to flip."

"I know what you mean," Hú Dié said. "I have built a few large delivery trikes for customers in China. I will be fine."

Hú Dié began to turn the cranks, and her taut biceps and triceps bulged out of nowhere as she made her way up the sloped driveway toward the road.

Peter glanced at me. "That girl is a rock."

"Actually, she's steel." Jake laughed. "Her name means Iron Butterfly in Chinese. Whatever you do, don't bump fists with her."

"I heard that!" Hú Dié shouted as she crested the driveway and turned right, heading up the hill.

I nodded at the road cycle. "Can I try that one now? I don't need to change my clothes."

"Be my guest," Peter said.

"Come on, bro," Jake whined. "Let me go next."

"Fat chance," I said as I put on my riding gloves and helmet.

"Promise me you'll take it easy," Peter said. "It's a bit more squirrely than the mountain cycle."

"Just like a regular road bike," Phoenix muttered.

"That's right," Peter said. "It goes with the territory. Speed comes at a price."

I climbed onto the bike and was surprised how comfortable it felt. The backrest went all the way up to my head. Peter strapped me in, one seat belt–like strap going around my waist while separate straps went around each ankle.

"This is my personal racing bike," Peter said. "You and I are about the same height, and our arms are about the same length. It should feel pretty good to you."

"It does," I said. "I could probably take a nap on this thing."

"Not while you're riding, you won't."

"I'm kidding."

"I know, but you need to be constantly aware on any bike, especially this one. You're very close to the ground, and I haven't outfitted it with a flag because I only ride it in races. Cars will have a difficult time seeing you."

"I'll keep my eyes peeled," I said. "I promise."

"All right," Peter said. "You want me to give you a push up the driveway? This thing climbs like a two-ton snail."

"Naw," I said. "If a girl can do it, so can I."

Peter chuckled. "If you say so."

"Hurry back, Beefcake," Jake said. "I want my turn."

Peter raised an eyebrow. "Beefcake?"

"Never mind," I said.

I began to crank, my hands revolving in unison. It was a strange sensation. It was more like rowing a boat than pedaling a bike. It was also hard work. I broke a sweat halfway to the top of the driveway, and by the time I reached the street, I smelled like the inside of a dragon bone container. Maybe this wasn't such a good idea, after all. I wasn't ready to tell Peter or Jake about the substance yet. I was going to have to buy some stronger deodorant, or maybe some cologne.

"Nice work!" Peter called out. "I guess those big guns of yours are good for something!"

I raised my hand and waved, but unfortunately the hand I'd raised also controlled the only brake lever. The bike veered left and began to roll down the steep street. Fast.

"Oh, crap!" I said. I found the brake lever and began to feather it, but it was too late. I had too much speed. I squeezed the brake lever hard, and the cycle began to skid.

"Ryan, look out!" Hú Dié shouted from somewhere behind me. She must have turned around and was now heading down the hill, too.

Ahead of me, a car was coming around the bend at the very bottom of the hill, between the stone seawall and the hillside.

I released the brake lever and turned the cycle hard in an effort to stop my skid.

Bad idea.

The trike toppled over and careened into the rocky hillside. My head smacked against the headrest, knocking my helmet over my eyes. I saw stars and tasted blood in my mouth. I must have bitten my tongue.

The trike somehow righted itself, and I scrambled for the brake lever, my helmet still over my eyes. I found the cranks, but the brake lever was no longer attached. I tried to throw myself free of the cycle, but I was solidly strapped in. The driver honked, and I heard tires squeal.

I was low enough to the ground that I could press my hands against the street, so I did. The padded palms of my riding gloves snagged and skittered over the rough asphalt as I pushed by entire body weight against my arms, but it was no use. In fact, it made matters worse. The cycle began to wobble, and it toppled over again as I reached the bend in the road.

I hit the low stone wall with a *THUMP* and the world went black.

9

"Are you alive?" I recognized Hú Dié's voice.

I opened my eyes to find her and a stranger staring down at me. I blinked, and Hú Dié smiled.

"Just a flash knockout," Hú Dié said. "He'll be fine."

"We don't know that," the stranger said. It was a middle-aged woman who looked vaguely familiar.

"Ms. . . . Bettis?" I said.

"That's right," Ms. Bettis replied. "Peter told me that you were coming to visit, but I hardly recognize you. You've . . . grown."

"Yeah," I said, shifting my weight so that I could unstrap myself from the custom racing handcycle that I'd just demolished.

"No, no! Don't move!" Ms. Bettis said. "I need to call an ambulance."

I thought about how dragon bone made me heal *like a mutant,* as Jake had said. I ran my tongue around the inside of my mouth and realized that it wasn't bleeding any-more. My gloves were shredded and appeared to be blood-stained, but my palms were dry. I balled my fists to hide the stains. The last thing I needed was anyone, especially paramedics, freaking out over my instant healing.

"I'm okay," I said, pushing myself up onto one elbow and quickly releasing the strap around my waist with my thumbs. "See?"

I unstrapped my ankles and rolled away from the trike. I stood, and my abdomen began to cramp. I didn't want Ms. Bettis to see me in pain, so I bent over and pretended to scratch my stomach.

"Feels like I've got a little road rash on my torso," I said, trying to make my voice sound normal. "All I need is a shower, and I'll be good as new."

"Are you sure?" Ms. Bettis asked.

"Positive. You live next door to Peter; come check on me anytime."

"I guess—" she said.

Ms. Bettis was interrupted by Jake and Phoenix hurry-ing down the street. Peter was ahead of them on a mountain cycle similar to the one Hú Dié was riding. He eased down the steep slope with far more agility and control than Jake and Phoenix, who were jogging in awkward, loping strides.

"Ryan!" Peter called out. "Are you okay? Why are you hunched over?"

"I'm fine," I said through gritted teeth. "Just a little road rash on my stomach."

"Whoa," Jake said, stopping before me. "Look at his brain bucket. It's toast."

"Good thing I've got a hard head to go along with a solid helmet," I said.

"You don't look so great," Peter said. "Kind of pale. Do you have double vision?"

"Yeah," Jake said. "How many of me do you see?"

"Fortunately, only one," I said.

Jake laughed.

"He sounds fine to me," Phoenix said. "He looks normal, too. Or as normal as an overdeveloped teenager can. The handcycle, not so much."

"I don't care about the cycle," Peter said. "It can be replaced. Ryan can't. Do you want me to call an ambulance, Ryan?"

"No," I said. "Ms. Bettis already offered. I'm fine."

"Let's get this mess out of the street, then," Peter said. "Phoenix, Jake—can you drag the handcycle up the street?"

"Put it in my trunk," Ms. Bettis said. "I'll drive it up the hill. I'll drive Ryan up, too."

"That's very nice of you," Peter said. "Thank you. Jake and Phoenix, this is my neighbor, Ms. Bettis. You guys load the cycle into her trunk. Hú Dié, will you help Ryan into her car, then *push* your mountain handcycle up the hill? I don't want any more accidents. I'll zip up to the house and pull together bandages, aspirin, and any other things I can think of that Ryan might need."

"I can think of a few things you might need," whispered Hú Dié with a grin as she helped me into the car. "Let's start with a lesson on how to ride a tricycle."

● ● ●

"Your stomach is cramping, isn't it?" Hú Dié asked.

I nodded.

Half an hour had passed, and I was lying on Peter's living room couch with my stomach still tied in knots. The rest of me was fine. Hú Dié and Phoenix were sitting with me, while Peter and Jake were in the kitchen.

"Is it bad?" Phoenix asked, his voice low.

"It's been worse," I whispered. "I think it wants to be fed."

Hú Dié shuddered. "That is so creepy. Do you need me to get some now?"

"Yeah. I'm due for today's batch. I usually take it in the evening."

"How much longer before you're done with it?" Phoenix asked.

"It could be a couple days, or a couple weeks," I said. "Your grandfather and Uncle Tí aren't sure."

Hú Dié glanced at my hands. "I hope you get over it soon."

"Why?" I asked. "Are you creeped out by my mutant healing powers?" I wiggled my fingers at her.

She wrinkled her nose. "No, you stink." She giggled.

I grinned, despite the painful cramping. She was right.

"Are you going to tell Peter and Jake?" Phoenix asked.

"I think I have to," I said.

"I'm not sure how I feel about that," he said.

"We can probably hide it for a little while," I said. "I don't feel like telling them right now, anyway. I feel awful."

"I'll be right back," Hú Dié said. "I'll go get the dragon bone."

"I'll come with you," Phoenix said.

"Hang on," I said, "I'm coming, too. Maybe I could help you assemble the bikes after you get the dragon bone. It might help loosen up my stomach."

"Sure," Hú Dié said.

I stood, and the three of us passed through the kitchen, into the garage. Thankfully, Peter and Jake were busy mixing up some chocolate protein shakes. I was starving.

Hú Dié opened the large bike frame box and separated the frames. Each one was wrapped in bubble wrap. She cut away the material covering my seat and grabbed a small wrench and a pair of needle-nose pliers. She used the wrench to remove the seat. Then she carefully removed a small bubble-wrapped object with the pliers. She handed it to me.

I unwrapped it and held it up. It was a stoppered vial of fine grayish powder.

"Dragon bone, all right," I said.

"Dragon *what*?" a voice replied.

Phoenix, Hú Dié, and I spun around to face the doorway. It was Jake.

10

"I said, dragon *what*?" Jake repeated.

None of us replied.

I looked from Phoenix to Hú Dié, then back to Jake, who was holding a tray containing three chocolate protein shakes.

Peter rolled up behind him.

"Dragon *bone*," Peter said. "Ryan said 'dragon bone.' What is that in your hand, Ryan?"

I stood speechless, my stomach cramping.

Hú Dié came to my rescue. "It is a . . . uh . . . type of dry lubricant," she said. "It is a Chinese product. I put it on all of my bike chains back home. I like it better than the grease most people use."

"Oh," Jake said. "Cool. Anybody want a shake?"

I sighed, grateful for Hú Dié's quick thinking. "I'll take one," I said. "I'm starving." I grabbed one of the large plastic cups and casually slipped the dragon bone into my pocket.

Phoenix and Hú Dié each grabbed a shake, and Jake disappeared into the house.

Peter rolled into the garage. "From what I can see through the bubble wrap, you guys have chosen some excellent bikes. Let me give you an overview of what we're going to do tomorrow. I've already told Jake. I'm going to teach you a few team drills, and I plan to digitally record them on cameras mounted on your helmets. I'd planned to ride alongside you with a camera on my helmet, too; however, I'm not sure I can get my road cycle in working order by tomorrow. The frame is cracked, and it's aluminum. I'd ride one of my mountain cycles, but they're too slow."

"I can fix it," Hú Dié said, "as long as you have the right welding rod and enough amperage."

"I was hoping you'd say that," Peter said with a grin. "You're sure you can do it?"

"Positive," Hú Dié said.

"Fantastic," Peter said. "Let's finish these shakes and get to work."

"You want us to assemble our bikes?" I asked.

"No," Hú Dié said. "I will do it while I am waiting for the welds to cool. You should relax."

"Yes," Peter said. "You and Phoenix are going to have to leave the garage now, anyway. I only have two welding shields, and the light from the welder will fry your eyeballs."

"Got it," I said.

"May I use your phone?" Phoenix asked. "I should call my grandfather."

"Of course!" Peter replied. "How foolish of me. I should have asked you earlier if you needed to use it. Feel free to call whomever, whenever. You too, Hú Dié, including China."

"Thank you," she said. "I will call later because of the time difference. My father will be sleeping now."

Peter nodded. "Ryan, have you called your mother yet?"

I shook my head. "I forgot to turn my cell phone on after the flight."

"You are so dead," Peter said.

"I'm on it," I said. "Come on, Phoenix. I'll show you where the phone is."

I called my mom from Peter's back porch. It overlooked the neighborhood below and the ocean beyond. It was spectacular. Plus, I could keep an eye out for Jake, who was somewhere inside. I didn't want him to hear any more talk about dragon bone, if the topic should come up.

My mom gave me a hard time for not having called her sooner, but she laid off me once I told her about my abdominal cramping and my wrecking Peter's handcycle. She gave me the typical mom-speech about being more careful, and I hung up, promising to keep her posted about my stomach and dragon bone in general. She was beginning to worry, and so was I. According to Uncle Tí and Phoenix's grandfather, I should have been seeing more improvements by now.

I went back inside and saw that Phoenix was still on the phone, so I went to find Jake. He was on the foldout couch in the guest bedroom, playing a video game on his tablet.

"What's up?" I asked.

Jake didn't reply. He was probably too busy with his game. I grabbed my tablet and flopped onto the guest bed.

I logged on to the Internet and decided to do a little surfing. I typed DRAGON BONE into my search engine, and to my surprise, I got a hit. I tilted my tablet so that Jake couldn't see it, and I hit the link. It was an online news article from a San Francisco Chinatown community newspaper.

SAN FRANCISCO, CA—CHINATOWN. A Chinese man was found dead of unknown causes yesterday in San Francisco's world-famous Chinatown. He has not been identified, but sources close to the investigation speculate that he is a member of one of China's notorious crime syndicates. Distinctive tattoos connect him with a particular sect of black-market operatives known for distributing medicinal contraband such as tiger and bear gallbladders, which are highly prized by certain traditional Chinese herbalists and apothecaries. Law enforcement officials disclosed that this individual was last seen the previous evening in multiple Chinatown apothecary shops inquiring about a little-known substance called dragon bone. Dragon bone is a legendary powder purportedly ground from the fossilized bones of dragons, though the medicinal benefits appear to have been forgotten over time. Anyone with information about this incident or dragon bone is urged to contact authorities immediately.

I swallowed hard and hit my browser's BACK button. Phoenix came into the bedroom.

"Ryan," he said, "can I talk to you for a minute?"

"Sure," I said. "I have some something to tell you, too. Let's go outside. I love that back porch."

"Don't bother," Jake said without looking up from his game. "You might as well just talk here. I know all about dragon bone. I can surf the Internet, too, you know. *Dry chain lube?* Give me a break."

Phoenix ran a hand through his hair. "Oh, man. What's on the Internet?"

Jake put his tablet down. "Show him, Ryan. I'm guessing that's what you were just looking at. Your face went all pale as you read it."

I looked at Phoenix. "I think we need to have a team meeting."

"That's what I came to tell you," Phoenix said. "Grandfather and Uncle Tí think we should get Jake and Peter up to speed as quickly as possible. There is some crazy stuff going down in Chinatown."

Peter had ordered a couple of pizzas after he and Hú Dié had finished in the garage, and it took the meal plus an entire quart of ice cream to tell him and Jake everything about dragon bone.

Peter remained quiet the whole time, and it was difficult for me to figure out what he was thinking. At first he looked skeptical, but after I took a dose of dragon bone and showed him how my cramped abs immediately loosened, it was clear that he believed me.

He seemed disappointed in me, too, and I couldn't really blame him. Thankfully, he offered to help. I don't know what I would have done if he'd turned his back on me.

It was one in the morning by the time we'd finished, and we did rock-paper-scissors to see who was sleeping where. I won and picked the twin bed in the guest room. Phoenix and Jake had brought sleeping bags and decided to share the pullout couch that was also in the guest room. Hú Dié got the regular couch in the room Peter used as an office.

I brushed my teeth and flopped into bed. I thought I'd have a hard time falling asleep, but as soon as Jake turned out the light, I crashed hard.

I was wakened by the sound of a whirring mixer. I rolled over and looked at the clock, shocked to see that it was eleven a.m. Phoenix and Jake were already up and gone.

My arms and legs were heavy, and my head was cloudy. I pulled on some sweats and dragged myself to the kitchen to find Phoenix and Jake sitting at the kitchen table with Peter. Hú Dié was beside the stove, mixing some type of batter.

"Good morning," Peter said. "How do you feel?"

"Ugh," I said. "Horrible. I don't have any energy."

"Sorry, bro," Jake said. "Do you think you can ride today?"

"Yeah, but don't expect me to pull you like I did the other day. I just don't have it in me."

Peter frowned. "It's the dragon bone, isn't it? Or lack thereof."

I nodded.

"I'm trying to get a handle on how much to work you today," Peter said.

"Have you changed your plan?" I asked.

"No, only refined it. Hú Dié is being kind enough to cook us some organic protein pancakes. After breakfast, Phoenix and Jake are going to do the dishes while Hú Dié puts some finishing touches on my bike and you help me hitch my old bike rack to my van. Then we'll load up the bikes and hit the road. I want to take a close look at each of your forms, as well as teach you guys a drafting drill or two."

"Sounds good," I said. "I'll feel better once I start sweating."

"About that," Peter said. "I noticed yesterday that your sweat smelled a little . . . off."

"It's the dragon bone. Hú Dié says I stink."

"I wouldn't exactly say stink," Peter said. "*Ripe* is a better word."

Hú Dié giggled.

Jake laughed. "Yeah, like a bad apple! I'll second that."

"Third," Phoenix said, "but I'm used to it. My grandfather has the same smell."

"Thanks, guys," I said. "Remember that when you're drafting off me today. I might even forget to put on deodorant, too, just for you, Jake."

"Gross, bro!"

It was well past noon by the time we arrived at our surprise training destination, which turned out to be Point Lobos State Reserve. It was only a few miles from Peter's house and I'd been there before, but I'd never considered it as a place to train. It was perfect for road bikes.

We passed through the entrance gate and drove along a smooth two-lane road that was free of potholes. It wound through tall, shadowy eucalyptus trees before crossing a prairie-like meadow and finally reaching the ocean. The road didn't stop at the water, though. It made a sharp ninety-degree turn to the left and continued along the water's edge. We followed it a short distance, and Peter turned off into a small dirt parking lot that faced the park's most famous attraction—the tidal pools. Rocks the size of houses were strewn along the shoreline.

Peter parked the van, and Jake said, "Check it!" He pointed to a wooden post that read BICYCLES.

Peter laughed. "That sign always cracks me up. I've never seen a single bicycle here. There are miles of trails, but most people hike them on foot or poke around here in the tidal pools. A lot of people scuba dive here, as well, though mostly in a cove down the road. This entire park is a marine sanctuary. It's considered by many to be the crown jewel of California's park system."

"I can see why," Hú Dié said. "It is so beautiful. I might have a difficult time keeping my eyes on the road."

"You better focus once you're on the bike," Peter said, his tone serious. It seemed we were done joking around for now.

After unloading, Peter strapped himself into his hand-cycle and sent us off to take a quick look at the tidal pools while he set up our helmet cameras. We didn't have to go more than a stone's throw.

The pools were quite close to the road, and they varied from the size of a basketball to the size of a basketball court. Most were formed by gaps between the massive rocks. A couple were pretty deep—I'd jumped into one on a visit as a kid and it was over my head; my mom had to help me climb out of it. Colorful creatures flitted among innumerable underwater crevasses, either swimming or scurrying across the slime-covered face of the scarred rocks.

"Wonderful," Hú Dié said after several minutes of slouching over three different pools. "I could stare into these all day."

"Me too," Phoenix said.

"Not me," Jake said, straightening. "This is boring, and that slime smells worse than Ryan's sweat. I'm going to see if Peter needs help." He walked off.

I shook my head. "I think I'll go back, too. I've seen these pools before."

"Fine," Phoenix said. "Let's help, too, Hú Dié. Maybe we can explore here some other time."

We got the cameras mounted and positioned; then we climbed onto our bikes and warmed up with some easy spinning on the flat coastal road. We didn't draft off of one another, and we weren't supposed to concern ourselves with form, technique, or positioning. Peter rode alongside us, his repaired handcycle working flawlessly and looking even better than it originally had. Hú Dié had done an amazing job.

It was a warm day, and after a few minutes I felt the first trickle of sweat run down my face. My body began to loosen up and I felt pretty good, though I guessed I only had about 50 percent of my normal energy level. We spun for another five minutes before Peter pulled us over into a different parking lot and had us get off of our bikes.

"Time to stretch!" he announced.

"Oh, man!" Jake whined. "I *hate* stretching! Why didn't we just stretch first and get it over with?"

"It's better to spin, then stretch," Peter said. "You'll get more out of it that way. Do any of you have a good stretching routine?"

"I have about a million," Phoenix said, "but they are all for kung fu. Is that okay?"

Peter shook his head. "I'd rather you guys stay away from kung fu. I remember Ryan's acupuncture story."

"I have one," Hú Dié said. "I teach it to people in our bike shop."

"Perfect," Peter said. "Lead the way, Hú Dié. I'll observe."

Hú Dié got down to business, starting us with some difficult stretches.

And then it got worse.

I'd done a ton of weight lifting, but I'd never been concerned about flexibility. Jake struggled even more than I did. He was generally pretty lazy. If he wasn't riding his bike, he was slumped on a couch somewhere playing video games. He couldn't even touch his toes.

People must be a lot more flexible in China because Phoenix and Hú Dié both excelled at stretching. Hú Dié looked like an Olympic gymnast, while Phoenix looked like a noodle. To say that Peter was impressed with those two would be an understatement. He asked Phoenix and Hú Dié to help me and Jake with our stretching, and they agreed, pushing and pulling us into painful contortions.

THE FIVE ANCESTORS OUT OF THE ASHES

Once Hú Dié finished abusing us, we remounted our bikes. Peter had us ride back and forth past him, both solo and as a group, so that he could observe and record our form and posture in detail. Next, we had to pedal with only one leg to give him a sense of how smooth our pedal stroke was or, in Jake's case, wasn't. I'd never noticed before, but Jake had a really sloppy cadence. Pedaling with one leg really showed whether or not you were efficient and if you used the entire range of motion to propel the bike. Jake pedaled like a preschooler, mashing down on his pedals with each revolution and never pulling up.

When Peter had seen enough, he sent us up the park road in a loose peloton, telling us to ride single file and at least five feet apart, which was too far to draft. He rode alongside us, shouting tips about drafting before we actually did it. It was like a moving classroom.

Then he had us tighten up, each front tire less than a foot away from the next bicycle and off to one side. I was in the lead, with Hú Dié behind me, then Phoenix, and finally Jake. The others hooted their approval as they began to draft off me and each other in sequence. It was a good feeling.

We reached a turnaround at the end of the road and snaked around two parked cars after a quick warning shout from me. The cars were empty, but I steered us well away from them, just in case. We breezed through the turnaround and headed back in the other direction, still in our tight peloton.

"You guys are doing great!" Peter shouted. "Let's practice falling off. Do you remember the signal, Ryan?"

"Yeah!" I shouted back. We'd just talked about it on the drive over here.

"Whenever you're ready, go for it!"

We were hugging the right side of the road, so I glanced over my left shoulder. The coast was clear. I stuck my left elbow out as a visual signal and shouted, "Falling off!"

"Falling off!" Hú Dié shouted back, acknowledging my verbal signal.

I accelerated to make sure I'd clear Hú Dié's front tire; then I veered to the left and tapped my brakes slightly so that the entire group could pass on my right. I pulled in behind Jake and locked onto his wheel, feeling my bike suddenly sucked forward. It was my first time drafting, and I hooted, too. It was neat.

We took turns falling off until Peter had plenty of footage.

"One more drill, and we'll call it a day!" Peter shouted to us. "I'll pretend I'm a car. You guys react. Do you remember the verbal signals we talked about?"

All four of us shouted, "Yes!"

"Do it!" Peter shouted, and slowed until he was behind us.

"Car!" Phoenix shouted from the back of the peloton. "Single up!"

"Single up!" we all shouted back, and we spread out in a single-file line to minimize the risk of possibly crashing into one another and to leave more space for the approaching vehicle to pass.

Peter shot past us as if we were standing still. I couldn't

believe how fast he had accelerated. His bike didn't have any more mechanical advantage than ours. I glanced at my bike's electronic display. It read fifteen miles per hour.

Peter was easily going twice that speed—with his arms.

We ran the car drill a few more times, rotating our positions within the peloton. Peter passed us on our final run-through when Hú Dié, who was at the end of the line, unexpectedly shouted, "Car! Single up!"

"Single up!" we all shouted, and we spread out, single file.

I was in the lead, and I glanced over my shoulder to see a car coming up behind us. Peter was about fifty feet ahead of me, matching my speed.

The car gave our peloton plenty of room as it eased past, which was nice for a change, but it slowed suddenly once it reached Peter. The driver had his windows down, and he began to wave enthusiastically to Peter.

Peter nodded back.

The driver then began to fumble around for something, causing his car to swerve.

I did my best to keep one eye on the road ahead of me and another on the swerving vehicle. Thankfully, the driver soon regained control of his car. Now holding a cell phone, he snapped Peter's picture. Then he eased off the gas and snapped pictures of me and the others. As he sped away, I noticed that the car had a handicap license plate.

We tightened our peloton back up, and Peter slowed until he was riding beside me.

"Who was that guy?" I asked.

"I have no idea," he replied.

We were nearing the van, and Peter announced that we were done for the day. It was time to warm down. We all shifted to low gears and began to spin like we did earlier. We reached the parking lot and climbed off of our bikes.

"Five minutes of stretching," Peter said. "Hú Dié, would you do the honors?"

"Come on, Coach!" Jake moaned. "You said we were done for the day."

"You'll live," Peter said.

"Everyone, follow me," Hú Dié said, and she led us through a short but grueling routine. She seemed to enjoy watching me and Jake writhe in agony, and Phoenix appeared to enjoy our pain, as well, as I caught him smiling more than once.

Back at Peter's house, we took turns showering, and then Peter set about making dinner. I hunkered down over my tablet to surf the Internet.

I did another search for dragon bone, but didn't get any more hits. Then, for the heck of it, I did a search for "Peter Hathaway." I'd Googled him several times before we came out here, and I was pretty familiar with most of the cycling forum and blog posts floating around concerning him. However, a new one popped up. It was from a handcycling forum, and it had been posted in the last few minutes. It read:

Yo, fellow hand-crankers! Guess who I just saw tearing up the pavement at Point Lobos today? None other than the great Peter Hathaway! Man, it was cool. It's no big surprise that he was tooling around on a sweet custom handcycle, but it looked as if he was coaching a team—of teens, no less! And one of them was a girl! How sweet is that? Coach

Hathaway, back in the training business! I like the sound of it. Here are a few pics!

Embedded in the post were several photographs that clearly showed Peter and the rest of us. While it was kind of creepy, it was also pretty cool. We looked like a real touring team.

"Hey, guys!" I called out from the guest bedroom. "Check this out!"

Jake poked his head in. "What's up, bro? Phoenix and Hú Dié are chilling outside on the porch."

I handed him my tablet.

"No way!" he said. "That's totally rad! Come on, let's show the others!"

We showed Phoenix and Hú Dié, and they thought it was as cool as Jake and I did. Then we all went into the kitchen and showed Peter, but he didn't think it was a big deal, probably because he was used to the attention. I emailed a link to the post to my mom, along with a link to the dragon bone article from last night, and we ate dinner.

By the time we'd finished doing the dishes, the cycling forum had more than a dozen comments about Peter and his "mystery teen team." Several of the forum members said that they had spread the news by forwarding a link to the post and pics to friends. It seemed that Peter was even more famous in the cycling community than I had imagined. It made me proud to be training with him, and even more proud that we were related.

I began to feel a little woozy and my abs started cramping, so I snuck off to take my daily dose of dragon bone while Peter connected his video playback system to the big-screen monitor in his living room. When I rejoined the group, everyone was lounging on Peter's large sectional couch.

I plopped down next to Jake. He was holding a huge bowl of popcorn. It made my stomach turn.

"How you feeling, champ?" Peter asked.

"Not too bad," I lied.

"You did well today," Peter said, "all of you. I'm going to enjoy reviewing the footage. Just sit back and relax while I talk us through it. I'll start with my recording. Then we'll fast-forward through each of yours, stopping only when I need to highlight something. It's going to take a couple hours."

Great, I thought. I wasn't sure I'd be able to stay awake that long.

Peter ran through everyone's footage, but he didn't have much to say about my technique. It was solid, thanks to the private coaching I'd had when I lived in Belgium with my uncle. Phoenix was pretty solid, too, and Hú Dié looked as if she'd been riding her entire life, which she probably had.

Jake, however, was another story.

"How long have you been riding, Jake?" Peter asked when we'd finished the last of the footage.

"I don't know," Jake said. "I think I learned to ride without training wheels when I was like four years old."

"No, I mean, when did you start racing mountain bikes?"

"A couple years ago."

"Had you ever raced any other kinds of bikes? BMX, maybe?"

"Sure."

"How did you do?"

"I used to smoke everyone!" Jake said. "I only stopped because the place where I used to race closed down. Why?"

"Because of your pedal stroke," Peter said. "When you race BMX, your feet aren't connected to the pedals, so you're always hammering down with your legs, never pulling up. Also, you don't change gears enough, which is also a throwback to your BMX days. BMX bikes only have one fixed gear. Despite these things, I understand that you usually do quite well in your mountain bike races."

"Yeah. I only lose to Ryan and Phoenix."

Peter smiled. "That just goes to show how much natural talent you have. You are a beast, Jake. With a little coaching, you just might catch these two."

Jake flashed a huge grin. "I did beat Phoenix once, but it wasn't exactly a race."

"I beat myself," Phoenix said. "I'd never ridden a road bike before. I burned out too soon."

"Knowing your limits is one of the most important aspects of cycling," Peter said, "particularly for sprinters. I'll help all of you with that."

"Sweet," Jake said. "Hey, is there any way you could give me a little extra coaching? Maybe during our downtime or something?"

"Be glad to," Peter said. He glanced at the clock and sighed. "Here we are, past midnight again. It seems you guys are night owls, just like me. Let's hit the hay and see what time we all roll out of bed. We can spend the first part of the day around the house, fine-tuning specific skills, and the latter part pounding the pavement. At night, we'll go over the footage. Sound good?"

We all nodded.

"See you in the morning, team," Peter said. "I'm really excited about tomorrow. You guys all have *serious* potential."

I was wakened by a gentle poke to the ribs from Hú Dié's steely elbow.

"Rise and shine," she said. "You look terrible."

I glanced at the clock and saw that it was ten a.m. I didn't feel the least bit rested.

I groaned as Hú Dié left, closing the door behind her. I dressed before stumbling to the kitchen, where she, Phoenix, Jake, and Peter were downing strawberry protein shakes. I hadn't even heard the blender.

"Whoa," Jake said. "You look like crap."

"Thanks," I said. "I feel like I look."

"Is there something I can do for you?" Peter asked. "Should I call your mom?"

"No," I said, and I grabbed a shake they'd poured for me. "I don't want her to worry. Hopefully, it will pass soon. If not, I'll try exercising. That usually helps."

I sat down and took a sip. I immediately felt a little

better. My body seemed to appreciate the sugar. "This is good," I said. "Who made it?"

"Me," Jake said. "Peter showed me his secret recipe. He used it when he trained for the Paralympics!"

"Awesome."

"He's also going to give me private coaching right after we finish our shakes. We're going to hook my bike up to his old-school stationary trainer. It's got rollers and everything!"

"Very cool," I said. "Are we going back to Point Lobos today?"

"Yes," Peter said. "We're leaving at five p.m. sharp. You're free to do whatever you'd like before then, within reason."

I turned to Phoenix. "What are you going to do?"

"Peter's got an old cyclocross bike in the garage," Phoenix replied. "Hú Dié is going to clean it up so that I can take it for a spin, but you could use it instead, if you want."

"No thanks," I said. "I appreciate the offer, but I'm not sure I could manage the neighborhood hills right now. I don't want a repeat of my handcycling performance."

Phoenix nodded.

"What are you going to do, Hú Dié?" I asked

"After I get the 'cross bike rolling, I am going down to the beach to practice some kung fu," she said. "You can come along, if you would like. I can show you some stretches to help with your flexibility."

"Kung fu?" I said.

"I know what Peter said yesterday," Hú Dié said, "but I think you'll be fine as long as you stay away from tai chi. What do you think, Phoenix?"

He shrugged. "He'll be all right, unless you start knocking him around again."

"She'll be nice," I said. "Won't you, Hú Dié?"

"I'll be nice to *you*," she said, sticking her tongue out at Phoenix.

Phoenix rolled his eyes.

"The beach sounds good," I said. "I could do some push-ups or something, too. Exercise always makes me feel better."

We finished our shakes, and Hú Dié headed out to the garage with Phoenix, Jake, and Peter. I went to the guest bedroom to grab my tablet. I did an Internet search for Peter's name and received an entire page of hits listing various cycling forum posts since last night. I clicked through most of them to find our photos and the same general story reposted, along with a wide range of speculations on who the "mystery teen team" was. It made me smile.

I then did a search for dragon bone but found nothing new. I checked my email and saw a reply from my mom:

Hey, kiddo. Thanks for the links! It's so nice that you and your friends are celebrities. How exciting! Who knows, maybe it will lead to something? A youth sponsorship, perhaps? Fingers crossed.

I don't know what to make of the dragon bone article. I've forwarded it to Phoenix's uncle and grandfather. I'll let you know if I hear anything from them. Have fun, and come home soon. I miss you. Love, Mom

Those last few lines kind of got to me. I realized that I missed her, too. I'd see her soon enough, though. Another seven days, and I'd be back in Indiana with only a few weeks remaining in our summer vacation. The summer was going by so fast.

"Ready?" Hú Dié asked.

I looked up from my tablet to see her standing in the doorway. She was digging grease out from beneath her fingernails with the corner of a shop rag.

"Ready," I said. I turned off my tablet and followed her out of the house.

"Peter told me about a staircase leading down to the water. It is supposed to be low tide, so we should have a little more sand than usual to stand on."

"I remember the stairs," I said. "It's great down by the ocean."

We found the staircase and descended to a patch of sand that wasn't much bigger than my backyard.

"This 'beach' used to be bigger," I said.

"It's fine," Hú Dié replied. "At least for what I plan to do."

"Me too. Are you going to stretch first?"

"Yes. Kung fu isn't like cycling. Stretching is the first thing you should do. You want to follow me?"

"No, but I will."

Hú Dié smiled. "I'll go easy on you. I know you don't feel well."

Hú Dié took off her shoes, so I did the same. Despite the warm air, the sand was chilly and damp. We began by flexing our toes and rolling our ankles. It seemed a strange place to start, but Hú Dié explained that we were going to stretch out our entire bodies, going from our feet all the way to our necks.

And we did.

It felt awesome. I kept waiting for my abs to cramp up, especially when I stretched my torso, but it was fine. This encouraged me to ask Hú Dié a question when we'd finished.

"Do you think maybe you could teach me a little kung fu? Just a punch or kick or something?"

"I thought you were going to do push-ups."

"I want to learn to do what you and Phoenix did in his grandfather's garage."

"That will take years."

"I've got to start somewhere," I said. "I promise I'll let you know if my stomach starts acting up."

Hú Dié thought for a moment. "We can try," she said. "Maybe Phoenix was right. You want to learn a Tiger style move?"

"Sure."

"How about a palm strike?"

"A palm strike?" I said. "Doesn't that hurt?"

"Not really. At least, not the person throwing it. The recipient might get a little sore, though."

"I won't break my hand?"

"You are far more likely to break your hand throwing a regular punch. There are many small bones in a fist that can easily break."

"I see."

"Drop down into a Horse Stance like Phoenix taught you."

I set my feet shoulder-width apart with my toes pointed forward; then I straightened my spine, bent my knees, and sank low.

"Perfect," Hú Dié said. "You are a natural."

I smiled.

"Seriously," she said. "Most people would have forgotten parts of that. You remembered everything. Now straighten your arms and raise both hands in front of you, chest-high, like this."

I copied her.

"Next," she said, "flex both wrists back so that your palms are facing forward. Spread your fingers out."

I did.

"Good," she said. "Finally, curl your thumbs and fingers inward. This is a basic tiger-claw fist."

"Cool," I said.

Hú Dié nodded. "You are going to strike with the heel of your palm. The support for the blow comes from your wrist and the forearm bones behind it. Never throw a regular punch with this kind of fist, though, or you will break your hand, for sure."

"Okay."

"Now," she said, "inhale deeply as you bend your elbows and retract your arms, stopping your raised palms on either side of your chest."

I did it.

"Finally, exhale and thrust your palms forward, aiming the heels of your palms at an imaginary target. It is very important that you exhale forcefully when you strike."

I exhaled as I thrust my arms forward, grunting with the effort.

Hú Dié smiled.

"How was that?" I asked.

"Not bad. I forgot to tell you that you can make some noise if you feel like it. It means you are giving it all you have. Do it again."

I raised my tiger-claw fists and inhaled, pulling them back to my chest; then I exhaled powerfully while thrusting the heels of my palms forward with all my might. This time, my grunt came out as a ROAR.

"Wow!" Hú Dié said. "Very intimidating! Just like when you ride. Keep practicing, but you do not have to get quite so into it. Maybe go back to grunting like you did the first time."

I nodded and wiped beads of sweat from my brow. The seemingly simple strike was turning out to be a lot of work. "This is great exercise. Thank you for showing it to me."

"My pleasure. Practice it two thousand times a day, and you will have it down in less than a week."

"Two *thousand* times? Are you kidding?"

Hú Dié shook her head. "There is a famous saying, 'I fear the person who practices one strike ten thousand times, not the person who practices ten thousand strikes only once.'"

"Good point," I said.

"If you truly do one thousand, nine hundred and ninety-eight more today, I promise I will teach you something else tomorrow. Make sure you alternate hands, though. Do one thousand with each. It sounds worse than it is."

"I'll do it."

Hú Dié smiled. "I think you are going to make a great martial artist, Ryan."

I beamed. "Really?"

"Well, you actually punch like a girl. We are going to have to fix that."

The next five days were more or less the same. We would wake up and do our own thing until late afternoon; then we'd train as a team at Point Lobos. Afterward, we'd watch the footage together.

True to her word, Hú Dié taught me five new kung fu moves, one each day: a hammer fist, a front kick, a side kick, a knee trap kick, and how to catch an opponent's kick like Phoenix had caught her kick at his house. The last two could only be done with a partner, so she worked with me. Hú Dié took quite a beating, as both moves involved my knocking her down in the cold, wet sand and twisting one of her legs into a pretzel. We switched legs to give me practice from both sides, and I could tell that she was still pretty sore from the routines. She was tough.

I was sore, too, but it was worth it. I was getting a great workout, plus I was beginning to feel like I could protect myself if I ever needed to. The dragon bone still seemed to have a stranglehold on my energy level, but at least it wasn't getting worse.

Jake continued to train one-on-one with Peter and made amazing progress. Everyone noticed it, and no one was more proud than Jake. It was cool to see. Peter only needed to show Jake something one time, and he never forgot it.

Phoenix spent his time alone on the 'cross bike, usually riding over to Point Lobos and tearing up the trails that allowed mountain biking. It was pretty obvious that he didn't like being on a road bike, but being out on the trails seemed to make him happy, so Peter let him ride that far on his own.

On our eighth night in California, we gathered as usual to watch the video, but Peter announced that he had other plans instead. There was something we needed to discuss.

"I have some exciting news for you guys," Peter said. "You all know that people are still gossiping on the cycling forums about you, right?"

We all nodded.

"Well," Peter said, "it looks like it may have amounted to something. There is an invitation-only twilight criterium in one week that will take place in downtown San Francisco. It's a race for adults, but all four of you have been invited."

Our jaws hit the floor.

"This is . . . incredible," Hú Dié said. "Even if none of us won, we would be sure to get attention. We could all find ourselves on teams."

"That's right," Peter said.

"Wait," Jake said. "What's a criterium?"

Peter laughed. "Sorry, Jake. It's a special kind of road

bike event that's usually quite short. A typical road bike race lasts several hours. The race usually begins in one place and ends in another. A criterium, or crit, takes place on a closed-loop course. It begins and ends in the same place, and usually lasts about an hour. It's basically a really long sprint. This one is a one-mile loop, and the race will run for one hour, plus three laps."

"How does that work?" I asked.

"After one hour, a signal is given. Whichever lead rider completes three full laps after the signal wins."

"Sounds simple enough."

"Yeah, they're very straightforward solo events. However, individuals sometimes work together as a team to improve their odds."

"Why did you call it a *twilight* criterium?" I asked. "They don't actually race at night, do they?"

Peter nodded. "They sure do. It's not as bad as you might be thinking. There are streetlights. I've raced in a few twilight criteriums before. They're a lot of fun."

"What about prizes?" Hú Dié asked.

Jake's ears perked up. "Prizes?"

"Most crits have stage prizes, or primes," Peter explained. "During certain laps, riders have the opportunity to win a prize if they win that particular lap. This race is special, so there won't be any stage prizes. However, there will be one whopper of a prize for the rider who crosses the finish line first—a professional cycling sponsorship!"

Phoenix's eyes widened. "Do you think any of us have a shot at winning it?"

"Honestly?" Peter replied. "It's a very long shot. The

race promoter is an old friend of mine and I told him as much, but he said that he didn't care. Your participation would help the event get more attention, and that's a priority for any promoter. I've already spoken with all of your folks, except yours, Hú Dié, and they support your participation and don't mind you staying out here longer. Additionally, Ryan's mother has finished her business in Indiana and has offered to fly out and help, which would be invaluable. While she doesn't ride, she has a deep knowledge of cycling strategy. She was instrumental in several of my victories in the past, particularly in criteriums. What do you say? Are you guys interested?"

"Yeah, baby!" Jake shouted.

"I'm in!" I said.

"Me too!" Hú Dié said. "I have plenty of time left on my travel visa."

We all turned to Phoenix. His face was somber, but then he broke into a huge grin. "I'm in, too."

"Yes!" Jake said, and he began to dance around.

Peter groaned. "You need a theme song to go along with that dance, Jake."

"How about 'Eye of the Tiger'?"

Phoenix, Hú Dié, and I replied as one: "No!"

We spent the rest of the morning making plans for the race. The fact that we would be competing against adults beneath streetlights began to wear on my mind, but it didn't bother me enough to make me want to back out. Plus, Peter promised to begin training us at night, which helped put me somewhat at ease.

Once I was able to push the night-racing concerns out of my mind, I realized I had a bigger problem—I was going to need more dragon bone. I didn't have enough to get me through the extra days. I thought my mom could bring me some, but she was worried about trying to get it through airport security.

Fortunately, Uncle Tí had me covered. He made a phone call to PawPaw, an apothecary friend of his in Beijing. It turned out she had a friend in San Francisco's Chinatown who could be trusted. Her name was YeeYee, which means "Auntie" in Chinese. Uncle Tí made arrangements to ship out a small amount of dragon bone via courier airplane as a medical necessity—which it was—and YeeYee was going to be able to pick it up at San Francisco International Airport, and we could get it from her. Sending it to her instead of Peter directly seemed best because she often received medicine from doctors. Additionally, she could check it over to make sure it hadn't been tampered with. Uncle Tí didn't want to take any chances.

I was also happy that my mom was coming to help us. She seemed more excited than I was, and I looked forward to learning all she knew about racing strategy. I'd had no idea her background was that extensive, and I felt closer to her than ever before.

Peter called the race promoter to confirm our participation, and almost immediately the cycling forums and blogs began to light up with news that the "mystery teen team" would be at the event. It was both exciting and a little scary for us. What it meant, though, was that we were going to have to practice like never before.

Since Peter was going to take us all to Chinatown tonight to pick up the dragon bone, we decided to head to Point Lobos early. We arrived around noon and parked in our usual spot in front of the tidal pools.

Jake said that the forks on his road bike had been acting a little strange the previous day. Hú Dié suspected a hairline weld fracture, but she hadn't found one. As a precaution, we'd brought along the 'cross bike for Jake to ride, if necessary.

We started with our usual spinning; then we stretched. The stretching routines were getting more difficult, but Jake and I were already seeing some serious results. While standing, I could almost put my palms flat on the ground, and Jake could now press his knuckles against the road. Peter was impressed.

We finished stretching, and Peter decided to begin our session with the "car" drill we'd practiced the first day. Peter once again played the role of the car as the cameras on our helmets recorded our every move. He was in rare form, zooming past us faster than I'd ever seen him ride.

When we reached the turnaround at the end of the road, I saw a pickup truck parked there. A man wearing a cowboy hat was behind the wheel, and a large dog sat beside him. I gave the others a warning shout, and we expertly avoided the vehicle as we came about in our peloton with Peter bringing up the rear. We began to head back in the opposite direction, when Peter suddenly surged forward, pretending to be a car once more. Hú Dié shouted, "Car! Single up!"

Jake, Phoenix, and I shouted back to confirm that we'd heard her. "Single up!"

We spread out, and Peter blew past us.

"Wow!" Jake shouted from behind me.

I glanced down at my electronic display: twenty-two miles per hour.

"What a maniac!" I shouted back with a laugh. "He has to be going at least forty miles per hour! I—"

"Car!" Hú Dié shouted again. "Single up!"

"Single up!" Phoenix, Jake, and I shouted back, and I glanced over my shoulder. The truck that had been parked at the turnaround was approaching us.

Fast.

We spread out and slowed. Ahead of us, Peter turned around in the very center of the road.

"Car, Peter!" I shouted.

Peter saw it, too. He began to crank for the opposite shoulder of the road to give the pickup plenty of space. I glanced back once again and saw that the truck was already beside Hú Dié. Phoenix was thirty feet in front of her.

The truck's horn blared, and I heard a dog howl.

My heart leaped into my throat.

I knew that howl. . . . It was a black mouth cur hunting dog from Texas named Bones.

"Phoenix!" Hú Dié cried. "Help!"

The horn blasted again, and Bones howled once more.

I started to turn around as the driver suddenly jerked the car's steering wheel toward Hú Dié, cutting her out of the peloton like a cowboy cutting a calf out of the herd. She screamed and veered across the road onto the narrow rock-strewn shoulder, the tidal pools only a few feet away from her. An instant later, she fell.

I cut across the road as the truck stopped and Bones leaped out of the vehicle's open passenger window.

"Bones!" the driver shouted. "Git back here!"

Bones ignored him.

Jake veered around and pulled up next to me.

"What's going on?" he shouted.

"I don't know, but that's Murphy's dog!" I shouted back. "Murphy was a bad guy down in Texas. The dog *hates* Hú Dié!"

Phoenix had turned, too, as Jake and I caught up with him, and Peter was not far behind.

The driver suddenly gunned the truck's engine, and the vehicle lurched toward us, head-on. Jake and I steered away, but Phoenix headed straight for the oncoming pickup.

"Phoenix, no!" Peter shouted, but Phoenix continued to hammer forward. When a collision seemed inevitable, Phoenix turned his handlebars hard toward the truck's driver's side. His bike whizzed around the vehicle, and Phoenix reached toward the open window.

The driver opened his door, which smashed into Phoenix's bike.

Phoenix grabbed the door for support as his bike fell away. Phoenix was hanging from the door as the truck continued down the road.

The driver cut the steering wheel hard, and the door slammed shut with Phoenix still dangling from it. Peter pulled up to Phoenix on his low-riding handcycle, and Phoenix loosened his grip on the door as if to drop into Peter's lap. However, the moment Phoenix's feet touched Peter's bike frame, Phoenix pushed off and sailed into the driver's-side window, falling across the driver's arms. The steering wheel slipped out of the man's hands, and the pickup careened off the road. With the brakes shrieking, the truck stopped on the wet rocks at the ocean's edge. I could see Phoenix kicking his legs as Jake and I steered our bikes toward Hú Dié and Bones.

The huge dog had Hú Dié backed up to one of the large, deep tidal pools we'd stared into earlier. Bones snarled and snorted, saliva dripping down his huge jaws. I rode straight toward the animal, unsure what I was going to do next.

Bones made my decision for me. He leaped at Hú Dié, and I bunny-hopped a row of rocks, going airborne. As Hú Dié jumped into the tidal pool to avoid Bones's attack, my front tire hit Bones in midair. The dog, my bike, and I sailed into the pool after Hú Dié.

SPLASH!

Seawater filled my nose and open eyes. I twisted my heels outward, releasing my feet from my pedal clips, and I clawed toward the surface. However, before my head even cleared the water, a powerful hand grabbed the back of my collar and began to pull.

It was Hú Dié. She was clinging to one of the rocks. She shoved me halfway up the steep, slippery side of the tidal pool, and Jake helped me crawl the rest of the way out. He let go of me, and as we gave Hú Dié a hand she shouted, "Jake! Get your bike!"

Jake had dropped his bike next to the pool. He shoved it toward Hú Dié as she scrambled up the rock. She began to remove the quick-lock front wheel as Bones attempted to climb out of the pool a few yards from us. He wasn't making much progress, though; his claws couldn't get a grip on the slime-coated rocks. Hú Dié got the wheel free and hurled it at Bones. The wheel bounced off the dog's front legs, and he howled in frustration as he slid back into the water.

I heard a *SNAP!* as Hú Dié broke the front fork clean off Jake's bike and rushed to the edge of the pool where Bones had attempted to climb out. She thrust the bike fork at the dog as though she were holding a sword and screamed like a banshee.

Bones paddled over to different rock and tried to scramble, but it was clear that he wasn't going to be successful. The rocks were too slick.

I glanced over at the pickup and saw that Phoenix and the driver were still struggling with one another on the front seat. Peter was on his handcycle, pulling the car's passenger door open.

"I can handle Bones!" Hú Dié shouted, still waving the bike fork. "Go help Phoenix and Peter!"

Jake and I ran over to the truck as Peter reached into the front seat. "Phoenix!" he shouted. "Give me some space!"

Phoenix pushed back out of the driver's-side window as Peter grabbed one of the driver's ankles and began to haul the man out of the truck. The driver wrapped an arm around the seat belt to anchor himself and opened the glove compartment with his free hand.

Even from where I stood, I saw the glint of metal.

"Gun!" I shouted.

Phoenix ran around the front of the truck, heading for the passenger side.

"Peter!" Phoenix shouted. "Give *me* some space now!"

Peter let go of the driver's ankle, and the driver tried to pull his leg back into the front seat, but he was too slow. Phoenix hit the open door with his shoulder, slamming it shut on the man's leg with a horrible *crunch*.

"Owwww!" the driver howled.

Bones mirrored the howl from the tidal pool.

Phoenix drove his fist through the open side window. *CRACK!*

The driver's body went limp.

Phoenix stepped back, pulling the door back open, and Peter hauled the driver's unconscious body out onto the wet rocks.

I called back to Hú Dié, "Are you still good?"

"Yes!" she shouted. "Bones can't get out!"

"Let us know if you need help!"

"I will!"

"Huh?" Phoenix said, standing over the man. "He looks just like—"

"Murphy from Texas," I said, getting a closer look. "I don't believe it. That's Bo, Murphy's brother."

"You *know* this guy?" Peter asked.

"Not exactly," I said. "His brother, Murphy, was the contractor who built my uncle's training facility."

"But Murphy died, right?" Peter asked.

"Yeah," I said. "But during construction, Bo helped him do electrical work at the training facility a couple of times. He was Murphy's hunting partner, too. They took that dog Bones out into the woods behind the site once and came back dragging a wild pig they'd killed with giant knives. That's what Bones was bred for, finding pigs and holding them until hunters could finish the job."

"Nasty," Jake said.

"That would help explain why the dog is with him," Peter said, "but what are they doing *here*? Why would they attack Hú Dié?"

"I have no idea," I replied.

"Find something to tie him up with," Peter said. "I'll call the police." He began to fish around for his phone in the zippered pouch attached to his cycle's frame.

Phoenix pulled a large knife from a sheath attached to Bo's belt and cut several sections of the truck's seat belts and started to bind Bo's wrists and ankles. Bo began to stir.

Peter found his cell phone. "I'll call the police now."

"No," Bo mumbled. "No . . . police."

Phoenix held his hand up to Peter. "Hang on. Don't call yet. Let's hear what he has to say." He looked at Bo. "Speak up."

"I said," Bo repeated, louder and clearer this time, "no police."

Peter scoffed. "You must be out of your mind. You attacked these innocent kids and—"

"Innocent?" Bo said. "You don't know them very well."

"But I've never even met you," Phoenix said, shocked. "What are you talking about?"

"I helped my brother wire the training facility's security cameras," Bo said. "Remember the remote feeds? I know for a fact Dr. V mentioned them to you. I had plenty of time to view the footage from that night before the police computer geeks got to it. I saw what went down." He paused dramatically. "And I edited out some important footage."

"We didn't kill Murphy," Phoenix said. "Lin Tan did."

"I saw that," Bo said.

Then he smiled. "I also saw you hide that big ol' stash of dragon bone in the protein powder container. Very clever. That's the footage I deleted before the police saw it. *I* still have a copy of it, though. Considering all the . . . interest that's beginning to brew over dragon bone here in California, as well as you all being celebrities of sorts now, I believe the authorities would be mighty interested in seeing that footage."

Phoenix frowned. "How long have you been following us?"

"Off and on since the police finished questioning me back home in Texas," Bo said. "You were easy to find and trail in Indiana."

"We don't have any more dragon bone," Phoenix said.

"I don't believe that for one minute," Bo said. "But I also don't care."

"Why did you attack Hú Dié, then?" I asked.

"I was just trying to git your attention. I didn't think she'd fall, and I sure didn't expect Bones to go after her like that. He must be holding some kind of grudge. If I wanted to attack you, I would have done it in Indiana."

"Then what *do* you want?" Phoenix asked.

"I want Lin Tan," Bo said, "and you're going to help me git him."

Phoenix's expression changed. "Where is he?"

Bo smirked. "You want him, too, eh, kid?"

"Never mind that," I said. "Why should we help you in the first place?"

"Because," Phoenix answered, "if we don't help him, Bo will blackmail us."

"Very good," Bo said. "I not only have the footage of Phoenix's dragon bone switcheroo, but I know *all* about dragon bone. And like I said, I know what went down at the training facility. Murphy and I were tight, and I miss him a lot. But I'm willing to forget *your* involvement in everything if you git me close to Lin Tan."

"How do we find him?" Phoenix asked.

"I read in some cycling forum posts that you all are signed up for that nighttime bike race in San Francisco next week. I'm bettin' Lin Tan will be there."

"Why do you think so?" I asked. "Last we heard, the police can't even find him. He's probably somewhere in China."

"I don't think so," Bo said. "One of the people Lin Tan was attempting to sell dragon bone to called me the other day, looking for my brother. The guy wanted more info on this seller, Lin Tan. According to this guy, Lin Tan is now running with some bad hombres in San Francisco's Chinatown—guys all tattooed up like carnival sideshow freaks. And supposedly he's coaching a team that's signed up for that race."

"But Lin Tan doesn't have any dragon bone to sell," Phoenix said.

Bo grinned. "You think you took it all? No, son. I suspect Lin Tan withheld a fair amount from Dr. V. He used it to entice a buyer for the rest of the supply that he was attempting to steal before you all stopped him. He went underground, but my gut tells me he's going to surface for that race. However, I can't exactly go waltzing in there with my guns blazing. Besides, he'll recognize me. I need you to lure him to a nice, quiet place."

"These kids aren't going to help you," Peter said.

I swallowed hard. "I don't know about this."

Bo's eyes turned cold and shifted my way. "No, Ryan?

Let me help make the decision easier for you. Murphy had friends. Lots of friends, and they all want justice. Lin Tan may have pulled the trigger, but all I have to do is mention that Phoenix and Hú Dié played a role, too, and the boys back home will want to see them hang just as high as Lin Tan. The only one standing between your friends and my friends is me, understand?"

I felt my shoulders slump. "I understand."

"Good," Bo said. "Now help me fetch Bones. Your priorities just shifted from winning that race to bird-dogging Lin Tan for me. You're going to flush him out, or else."

STAGE THREE

ECHELON:

A line of riders taking orderly turns at the lead so that each rider will get maximum protection

We were so exhausted by the time we returned to Peter's
house, we didn't even unload the bikes or our gear. We'd
fished Bones out of the tidal pool, as well as my bike. Hú
Dié stayed well clear of the dog, and she didn't seem to
relax until we were safely inside Peter's house with the
doors locked.

We made phone calls to Indiana to let everyone know
what had just happened with Bo. No one could agree on
how we should handle the situation. Uncle Tí and my
mother wanted to call the police and let them sort everything out, regardless of the dragon bone consequences.
Phoenix and his grandfather, however, were determined to
try to keep a lid on the situation. And though I found it
difficult to believe, they favored helping Bo. Hú Dié also
seemed strangely eager to find Lin Tan, and my guess was
that she wanted to warn him about Bo. Lin Tan had shot
Murphy in order to save her and Phoenix, and she had even

planned to run off with Lin Tan at one point. It was all so complicated.

The only decision Jake and I made was to make no decision at all. In the end, we all agreed to discuss everything again in the morning. Bo had given me twenty-four hours to check in with him, so we had at least that much time to figure something out.

After the phone calls, I fell into my usual post-ride routine of rehydrating and surfing the Internet while waiting for my turn to take a shower. I found a ton of forum posts mentioning our being invited to race for a potential sponsorship. I still couldn't believe we'd gone viral without actually having done anything. All this from a random guy snapping a few pictures of Peter and us and posting them.

I also found an article about some recent cyclist deaths in the area, and I shared the article with everyone:

San Francisco, CA—Autopsy results have just been released as part of an investigation into the death of a Menlo Park semiprofessional cyclist, Jim Millar, who was struck by a vehicle while riding near his home three days ago. The county coroner determined that the collision was not the cause of death, and all pending charges against the driver have been dropped.

Millar, a locally known road bike racer, died of a heart attack that led to the collision. This corroborates the stories of the driver and numerous bystanders who witnessed Millar's sudden, erratic veering into the path of the vehicle. This is the third heart attack suffered by an accomplished road cyclist in as many months, leaving many to question why these top-level athletes who were apparently in peak physical condition would all die of similar causes in such a seemingly narrow time frame. The prevailing belief among Internet conspiracy theorists is that a mysterious gray Chinese powder that recently surfaced in San Francisco's Chinatown is to blame; however, investigators are quick to point out that no trace of any foreign substance has been found in any of the deceased. Two of the three riders were known to have consulted with Chinese herbalists at some point within the past six months. While no concrete link between the riders currently exists, investigators are handling all three deaths as though they are related. Watch our news feed for continuing developments.

We didn't know what to make of this latest story. Neither Phoenix nor I had ever heard of dragon bone triggering a heart attack in someone, but that didn't mean it wasn't possible. We called Uncle Tí and Phoenix's grandfather, but they'd already heard about it from PawPaw in Beijing. Finally, I sent my mom the link.

When we'd all finished getting cleaned up, we had a meeting to decide whether we should head to Chinatown as planned. My *dan tien* was absolutely screaming for more dragon bone, and I was nearly out. I thought it might be too late to drive the two hours there and then back again tonight. However, Uncle Tí assured us that the apothecary shop we were going to visit would definitely be open when we got there. He said that he'd make a call to let PawPaw's friend YeeYee know that we were on the way.

We arrived in Chinatown just as the sun was going down. There were cars and people everywhere. We eased past the famous Dragon Gate entrance at Grant Avenue, and Peter luckily found a parking spot on a nearby side street. It was hilly here, especially up Grant Avenue. There was no way Peter would be able to get around in his wheelchair right now. I tapped him on the shoulder.

"It's pretty crowded, Peter. How about you and I wait in the van while the others go get the dragon bone?"

"How far is the apothecary shop?" he asked.

I glanced down at the map on my phone. "Several blocks uphill."

"Maybe we could come back another time, like early morning."

I shook my head. "I can't wait much longer. Besides, we need to practice. We can't afford to waste half a day coming back."

Peter sighed. "You're right. I'll stay here. However, I'd feel better if you went with the others. Phoenix and Hú Dié may know how to take care of themselves, but you're a walking visual deterrent."

Jake laughed. "Ha! You—"

I raised a tiger-claw fist. "Don't even go there, Jake. He's talking about my size."

Jake clamped a hand over his mouth, still laughing.

Hú Dié rolled her eyes at Jake. "I think you should come with us, Ryan."

"Me too," Phoenix said.

"Peter, are you sure?" I asked.

"Get out of here," Peter said. "Do you have your cell phone?"

"Yep," I replied, "and I have your number programmed in."

"Call me if you run into any trouble. I plan to stay in the

van, but if you're gone longer than my stomach can tolerate, I'll be in one of these nearby restaurants. The food in most of these places is fantastic."

"Can we all grab something to eat before we head back to your house?" Jake asked. "I'm kind of hungry, too."

"Of course," Peter said. "A trip to Chinatown wouldn't be complete without a meal. We'll figure something out."

I nodded to Peter and stepped out of the van. The scent of fried food and car exhaust flooded my nostrils. Hú Dié, Phoenix, and Jake climbed out after me, and the four of us headed toward the Dragon Gate. As we neared it, I saw that it was actually three gates, with one large gate in the center for cars and a smaller gate on either side for people to walk through. They were all built of rectangular stones, and each gate had its own ornate roof covered with green tiles.

I looked up at the center gate's roof, where two golden dragons stared at each other. They appeared as though they were about to fight, perhaps over the golden ball between them. We stopped before one of the side gates, and on the ground at the outside corner was a stone statue the size of a large dog. I couldn't identify the creature, but it had a paw resting on a large stone ball.

Hú Dié walked up to the statue and patted it on the head. She looked at me and said, "This is Shishi. Do you know her?"

"No," I said. "Should I?"

"Yes," Hú Dié said. "She is a guardian. Some people believe that she is a dog, but most consider her to be a lion—just like you."

Jake laughed. "Ryan 'The Lion' Vanderhausen. If you ever become a mixed martial arts fighter, you'll already have a sweet name!"

I shook my head.

Jake pointed to the stone statue next to the pedestrian gate across the street. "Hey! There is another one. What's its name?"

"That is also Shishi," Hú Dié replied, "but that one is male. See how his opposite paw is raised? Some people believe that his ball represents the earth." She nodded toward the sphere beneath the raised paw of the lion by us. "Look at this one."

"It's a Shishi cub, lying on its back!" Jake said.

Hú Dié nodded. "That is how you know this one is the female. She represents life."

"Nice," I said.

"Come on," Jake said. "Let's get moving so we can eat." He passed through the small gate in front of us. Phoenix and I followed him. Hú Dié, however, went out of her way to walk through the large gate designed for cars.

Phoenix rolled his eyes.

"Why did she do that?" Jake asked. "Does she think she's a truck?"

"No," Phoenix said. "The large gate is traditionally reserved for important people. The smaller gates are for commoners—like us."

Jake laughed. I did, too. Hú Dié flashed a big grin.

I looked back and nodded at the golden dragons atop the center gate. "What do those represent?"

"I am not sure," Hú Dié said. "Dragons are complex creatures. They can mean many things."

"They look like they're ready to fight," Jake said, punching the air a few times. "What would happen if one of those dragons went toe to toe with one of the lions?"

"I suppose the dragon would win," Hú Dié said. "Dragons are believed to be all-powerful. What do you think, Phoenix?"

"If it were a kung fu fight," Phoenix said, "yeah, the dragon would win."

I thought about the dragon bone inside me. "If a dragon is all-powerful, can it ever be defeated?"

"The only thing that can defeat a dragon is another dragon," Phoenix said.

I sighed. I was a lion trying to defeat a dragon. I didn't stand a chance.

We headed up Grant Avenue, past rows of neon Chinese signs sticking out from stores along the hilly sidewalk. Lanterns hung from lampposts, and colorful banners were strung across the road.

The deeper we walked into Chinatown, the busier it got. It also became more foreign to me, looking more and more like a scene from a cool Hong Kong movie. The buildings rose higher, with balconies covered in drying laundry. It appeared that these buildings contained shops on the ground floor with residences above. The streets grew even more crowded, and the constant banter of Chinese grew louder.

I used to think Chinese things were cool, but being

surrounded by so much of it now made me uneasy. It reminded me of just how different the world was where I grew up, and it made me feel like I had no business being here or taking dragon bone in the first place. I wanted nothing more than to get what we'd come for, then get out of here as quickly as possible.

We pressed on until Hú Dié stopped in front of a large apothecary shop. I checked the map on my phone

"This isn't it," I said. "We're close, though. It's on Waverly Place." I showed her the phone.

"Follow me," she said.

We formed a tight peloton as if we were on our bikes, and Hú Dié led us into a dark side street. I had to shoulder my way through a group of rude guys who were just hanging around, doing nothing in particular. They wouldn't even acknowledge our presence.

"Keep your eyes open," Hú Dié whispered. "They seem like they're ignoring us, but trust me, they're watching our every move."

I checked to make sure my wallet was still in the front pocket of my cargo shorts, and I gripped my phone tighter, glancing at its display. We'd supposedly arrived at our destination, but I didn't see any storefronts. There weren't any signs, either.

Above us, a woman's voice rang out in Chinese-accented English. "Phoenix? Ryan?"

We glanced up into the darkness to see the outline of a person on a balcony.

"There is a door twenty feet ahead of you, on your left," the woman said. "Come up to the third floor."

We found the door and went up the narrowest set of stairs I'd ever seen. The treads were covered with cracked tiles, and my shoulders rubbed both tile-covered walls. I had to lower my head at the top of each flight of stairs to keep from banging it against the crumbling plaster ceiling.

"Who built this place?" Jake asked. "Elves?"

We reached the third floor and found an open door. An old woman stood in the doorway, dimly illuminated by a bare electric bulb. She wore a white silk robe and stood erect as a soldier. Her hair was long and gray with streaks of brown, and her bright eyes scanned each of us intently. She bowed slightly and said, "Welcome Ryan, Phoenix, Hú Dié, and Jake."

We returned her bow, and I said, "Nice to meet you, Ms. YeeYee."

The woman shook her head. "YeeYee is the name I reserve for strangers. You are not strangers. My name is Hok. Won't you come in?"

16

Wait! I'd heard the name Hok before, but I couldn't remember where. Jake and I took a step toward the old woman's door, but Hú Dié and Phoenix didn't follow. Their feet appeared to be glued to the floor. Hú Dié gaped at Hok, and I thought Phoenix's eyes were going to pop out of his head.

"You are *Hok*?" Hú Dié asked. "As in the Five Ances—"

Hok raised her hand, a hint of a smile on her lips. "Inside, dear. We have much to discuss."

The Five Ancestors! I thought. *Of course!* That's where I'd heard Hok's name. When Phoenix told Peter and Jake about dragon bone, he'd mentioned the Five Ancestors, five kids who changed the course of China's history almost four hundred years ago. One of them was supposedly Phoenix's grandfather. His name was Seh, or *Snake*. There was also a girl named Hok, or *Crane,* who used to pretend to be a boy. This was getting crazier every minute.

Hú Dié and Phoenix finally got moving, and we stepped

into an incredible room—from floor to ceiling, the walls were covered with wooden drawers. Some were large, like you'd find in a dresser, but most were tiny. They didn't look like they'd hold much more than a pill bottle. Each drawer was labeled with Chinese characters painted in gold. And then I noticed the smell. The room smelled . . . ancient. An earthy combination of odors wafted out from the drawers' unseen contents.

Hok locked the door behind us. "Where is Peter?" she asked.

"Too crowded for him out there," I replied. "Also kind of hilly."

"Of course," Hok said. "We'll try not to make him wait long." She came to stand next to me, and my *dan tien* began to quiver. I smelled something ancient about her, too— dragon bone. That would explain how she'd managed to live all these years.

"Few people know my secrets," Hok said to us. "My dear friend PawPaw does, as does old Long at Cangzhen Temple. However, Phoenix's grandfather Seh and Phoenix's uncle Tí are now just beginning to suspect my identity. I can't say that I haven't enjoyed keeping my existence a secret from Seh all these years. Perhaps if he was not so secretive him- self, I would have made myself known generations ago."

"Can I tell him?" Phoenix asked. "He's mentioned you a few times since I returned from China. I think he'd like to see you again."

"If he asks you directly about me," Hok replied, "then tell him what you know. Otherwise, I would prefer to tell him myself. I have a feeling we may be finding ourselves in need of a reunion soon. Dragon bone is rearing its ugly head again. Someone is going to have to put it to rest, for good."

I remembered what Hú Dié said back in Phoenix's garage about Phoenix being trained as a one-man army. I felt chills run up and down my arms.

"Who else knows about dragon bone?" Phoenix asked.

"Nearly everyone in Chinatown, it seems," Hok said. "Many months ago, a bicycle racer named Lin Tan went to every apothecary shop, asking if anyone had some for sale. Then a few weeks ago, he was back, asking if anyone wanted to buy some. No one took his offer seriously, except a local criminal leader named DuSow. They appear to have struck some kind of deal, as the two of them have been seen about Chinatown's underground together. I am beginning believe that Lin Tan was telling the truth about having dragon bone for sale, as PawPaw and Long informed me that some of their dragon bone had been stolen by someone fitting Lin Tan's description. Moreover, DuSow would not be fooled by fake dragon bone. He is one of the few people who know its true power."

"DuSow?" Phoenix said. "Does that mean *Poison Hand*?"

"Yes," Hok said. "It is a rare and terrible form of kung fu."

Phoenix nodded. "What do you mean that DuSow knows dragon bone's true power?"

"I have apothecary friends who believe that DuSow consumes dragon bone. I believe this may be true, as well. He has come to me over the years, looking for one rare herb or another, and he claimed to have known people who died a hundred years ago or more. From his detailed descriptions, it seems he was telling the truth. He looks perhaps fifty years old, but I would not be surprised if he was one hundred fifty."

Phoenix shook his head. "My grandfather told me that he, PawPaw, and Grandmaster Long stockpiled all of the remaining dragon bone in China."

"China is a big place," Hok replied. "They clearly missed some. Besides, a certain amount was shipped out of the country. Take me, for example. I left China to marry a young Dutchman. I took crates of medicinal herbs with me, including a fair quantity of dragon bone. I had used the substance once to heal my temple brother Ying. It worked wonders for him, as well as others I went on to heal with it. However, once I began taking it to extend my own life, I stopped treating others with the substance because I became keenly aware of the side effects. When I came to America a hundred thirty years ago, I brought my dragon bone with me, as well as all my other herbs."

Jake glanced around the room. "Wow. I guess that's how you had time to collect all this stuff."

Hok smiled. "I will take that as a compliment. I possess items that are but legends to most apothecaries."

"I didn't see any signs for your shop," I said. "How do people know where to find you?"

"Those who need me know how to find me," Hok said. "I have been here a very long time and have no need to advertise."

I thought about the gang in the street. "What about the guys hanging out in front of your building?" I asked.

"They know me. I daresay they keep an eye out for me,

too. While I don't normally associate with their kind, I have healed more than my share of them after they have been wounded in one skirmish or another. This is my home, as well as my shop. My doors are open to everyone, and I heal whomever I can, no questions asked. I charge no fee for my services, but most people do not leave without repaying me in some way. Just look at these walls. I once healed a carpenter's daughter, and he spent years returning here with his tools and scraps of wood, piecing together the most wonderful apothecary drawers I have ever seen. I have been very fortunate."

"I don't know how I'll be able to repay you," I said. "Maybe my mom can send you a check."

Hok shook her head. "I do not accept money. A phone call once you finally break your bond with dragon bone will be repayment enough. Phoenix's uncle has apprised me of your attempts to break your bond with dragon bone to date."

She paused.

"If I am to be honest with you," Hok continued, "I am concerned. He has done an excellent job formulating a plan for you, and considering the amount of exercise he tells me you have been getting, I would have expected the bond to be broken by now. I suspect your uncle gave you far too much. How do you feel at the moment?"

"Exhausted," I said. "But we had an intense day of riding earlier."

"Phoenix's uncle told me about what happened on your ride," Hok said. "We will concern ourselves with this 'Bo' person later. How is your *dan tien*? Does it seem active?"

"It quivered when you stood beside me and I smelled dragon bone."

"Oh, dear," Hok said. "It has taken root deeper than I was led to believe."

I swallowed hard.

"Is he going to be okay?" Hú Dié asked.

"Time will tell," Hok said. "But I fear time and exercise alone may not be enough."

"What else can I do?" I asked.

Hok stared, unblinking, at me. "There is a legend . . . of an antidote."

I felt my heart skip a beat. "Really?"

"Like so many things, it has been forgotten," Hok said. "I do not even know if it is real, but I have the ingredients listed somewhere. Let me find it."

Hok began to dig through some of the larger drawers. They appeared to be filled with scrolls.

"It is here somewhere," Hok said. "The antidote was developed for use on patients who took dragon bone for too long a period of time, either accidentally or intentionally. If I remember the tales correctly, the primary ingredient is a powerful poison that kills the dragon bone, for dragon bone is a living thing. There were stories of the antidote being worse than the dragon bone itself, though, and some people who took the antidote died from the treatment. Whether the deaths came from the antidote being mixed incorrectly, or from its simply being deadly, I cannot be sure."

"Maybe you should just skip the antidote for now," Jake suggested.

"We must explore every option," Hok replied, "even if we choose to not pursue it. Ahhh . . . here we are." She held up an ancient parchment that was rolled and tied with a bloodred ribbon. "Follow me."

Hok led us down a narrow hallway into a small kitchen. She unrolled the scroll on her kitchen table, and we all gathered around. The scroll was written in Chinese. Jake and I glanced at each other and shrugged our shoulders.

"*Long She?*" Hú Dié said, pointing to a Chinese character. "*Dragon Tongue?*"

"Yes," Hok said. "That is the poison."

"I get it," I said. "It takes a dragon to defeat a dragon."

"Exactly," Hok said. "Except in this case, 'dragon tongue' is actually the prepared skin of a poisonous toad. The toad is boiled and the skin cut into strips. The strips curl up when they dry, resembling a dragon's tongue. When reconstituted in a liquid, a very small amount is lethal. I do not have any, nor do any of my friends. It is primarily used by Poison Hand practitioners."

"Like DuSow," Phoenix said.

"Yes," Hok said.

"Huh?" I said. "What is Poison Hand kung fu, exactly?"

"Poison Hand kung fu practitioners make their hands toxic to others by soaking their hands daily in increasingly more potent poison," Hok said. "They grow immune to the poison because they begin their exposure in small amounts and increase the exposure over time. After years of this, a mere brush of a practitioner's hand against the skin of a non-practitioner leads to instant death. Other pores on the practitioner's skin are toxic, as well, particularly the skin of the forearms. However, the hands contain the highest concentration of poison. Practitioners must wear gloves in order to prevent themselves from accidentally poisoning everyone they come in contact with."

"People actually *do* this to themselves?" Jake asked.

"DuSow has," Hok said. "I have seen the aftermath of his tirades. That is another concern with Poison Hand kung fu practitioners—the poison eventually reaches their brain and makes them insane. I knew of another Poison Hand kung fu practitioner when I was a girl. His name was HaMo. He had lost at least as much of his mind as DuSow has, if not more. DuSow claims to have been a protégé of HaMo, but who knows whether there is any truth to that. I had thought HaMo died."

"What does *HaMo* mean?" Jake asked.

"Toad," Hok replied.

"What's up with all the animal names?" Jake said.

"Chinese animal names represent a person's kung fu style spirit. It is usually a nickname, but in some cases, like my name, Hok—or Crane—the given name and the nickname are one and the same."

"Like Ryan 'Lion' Vanderhausen," Jake said.

"Yes," Hok said, glancing at me. "That seems appropriate. Ryan does remind me of my old temple brother Fu—Tiger."

"I wish I had an animal name," Jake said.

"Sorry," Phoenix said. "There's no such thing as Laughing Hyena style kung fu."

Hú Dié and I chuckled, and Jake did, too. However, Hok eyed Jake intently.

"Right *order*, wrong *family*," Hok said, "at least scientifically speaking. Jake seems to be more like a jackal—clever, swift, and I'm willing to bet, sneaky."

"Yeah!" Jake said. "Exactly! Ah, except for the sneaky part, I mean."

"Truly?" Hok asked, still eyeing him.

"Well," Jake said, "kind of. Sort of. I don't know. Whatever. I still like the name: Jake the Jackal. So, who's going to teach me some Jackal style kung fu?"

"No one," Phoenix said. "There is no such thing."

"You could teach him Dog style kung fu," Hok said.

Hú Dié rolled her eyes. "Oh, great."

"What?" Jake asked.

Phoenix shook his head. "Another time, Jake. I don't feel like explaining Dog style kung fu right now. We have more important things to discuss, like Lin Tan. Do you know where to find him?"

"No," Hok replied, "and do not go looking for him. He belongs to DuSow now, and DuSow is not someone you want to upset. He is a powerful criminal with a vast network."

"Does he sponsor a team of road bike racers?" I asked. "We heard that Lin Tan is coaching a team here."

"That is possible," Hok said. "Many of DuSow's henchmen have heavily tattooed arms. I have heard of two tattooed Chinese men cycling about Chinatown recently with two nontattooed men who speak French."

"They could be from Belgium," I said. "Half the country speaks French. Lin Tan might even have recruited some of my uncle's team members."

Hú Dié nodded. "Also, do you know anything about the local cyclists with connections to Chinatown apothecaries who have been dying?"

"I do," Hok replied. "There were two apothecaries who had cyclists as patients. Neither of them prescribed dragon bone. Indeed, neither of them even knew what dragon bone was until the deaths. Neither had had any contact with the deceased cyclists for nearly six months, so the cyclists had both likely gone to some other apothecary, though I don't know whom. If DuSow has dragon bone, he would never sell it for any price."

"What if someone synthesized it?" I asked.

Hok paused. "Do you mean *manufactured* dragon bone?"

"Yes," I said. "That was my uncle's ultimate goal."

"I remember he said that," Phoenix said. "He had those fossils and that equipment."

Hok stared, unblinking, at me. "What equipment?"

"I remember a kiln and a vacuum pump," I said.

"What kind of fossils?"

"Some kind of dinosaur. Lin Tan got them."

"Lin Tan likely got those fossils from DuSow," Hok said. "DuSow is famous for illegally selling dinosaur fossils from China. Many people believe that dragons were some kind of dinosaur. A manufactured version of dragon bone would interest DuSow greatly. Something he could sell, potentially in very large quantities."

"*Can* dragon bone be manufactured?" Hú Dié asked.

"Not that I am aware of," Hok said. "True dragon bone

is a high-quality powder. There are no impurities. There was a rumor centuries ago of a man who attempted to make it by building an oven and baking fossilized dragon bones at a very high temperature under pressure. From what I recall, that man did make a substance very similar to dragon bone, though it was believed to contain impurities because it was very dark gray in color. He successfully consumed it for a time, experiencing increased physical strength and stamina. However, he soon died of the same affliction as the cyclists—his heart appeared to have stopped. In his case, it was shortly after a particularly grueling kung fu fight."

"Yeah," I said. "The cyclists all died while riding. Maybe they were pushing themselves really hard."

"That could very well be," Hok said. "The fact that the old rumor always made note of the kung fu fight has made me wonder if there was some type of ticking clock—a connection between impure dragon bone and a user overexerting himself. I'll make some inquires. In the meantime, it is getting late. You have given me much to think about. Let me retrieve your shipment, Ryan, and then you can be on your way. I would enjoy it if you would remain in contact with me. If I can assist you in any way, do not hesitate to ask."

"I will," I said. "Thank you."

"You are most welcome," Hok said. "I'll show you out."

We followed Hok back into the room with all of the drawers, and she opened a seemingly random one. She pulled out one of Uncle Tí's stoppered vials containing gray powder. Hok handed the vial to me, and I shoved it into one of my cargo pants pockets.

"Take great care with that," Hok said, "especially in Chinatown."

I nodded. "Thanks again."

"My pleasure," Hok replied.

The four of us bowed to Hok, and she returned the formal goodbye. We hurried down the low, narrow stairway and into the side street. When we approached the guys who were standing around earlier, they parted for us to pass without issue. I glanced up at the row of third-floor balconies and saw Hok's shadow staring down at us.

When we got to Grant Avenue, I called Peter, but he didn't answer.

"That's strange," I said.

"He probably left the van and did not hear it ring," Hŭi Dié said. "Chinatown can get quite loud."

"Let's go check," Jake said. "If Peter's not there, we'll go peek in some restaurant windows."

"Peek in windows?" I said. "Spoken like a true sneaky jackal."

Jake grinned.

We soon arrived at the van, but Peter wasn't there. He was probably eating somewhere nearby, most likely within sight of the van. Our bikes were still locked to the back, and this didn't look like the best neighborhood.

We walked over to the nearest restaurant, a small place with whole roasted ducks and chickens hanging in the window. We peered inside, but Peter wasn't there. The place next door had pictures of desserts plastered along the front windows and across the glass door, as well as images of smoothies and boba "bubble" tea.

"Maybe he just grabbed something to drink," I said, pointing to the pictures.

We peeked through the windows of that restaurant, too, but Peter wasn't there, either.

The next restaurant was across an alley. As we stepped off the curb, we avoided some kind of sludge that appeared to be thickened frying oil. It was slick and disgusting . . . and rutted with a pair of skinny parallel tire tracks. Several sets of footprints flanked the tracks.

"Peter's wheelchair!" I said.

"Call him again," Phoenix suggested.

I redialed Peter's number, and we immediately heard a faint ringtone at the far end of the dark alley. The ringtone abruptly stopped, and someone barked an order in Chinese. My cell phone display changed to CALL ENDED.

The four of us glanced at one another, and we headed into the blackness.

17

As we slunk down the dark alley, Jake whispered, "That sounded like Chinese. What did the guy say?"

"He said, 'Put him in the truck,'" Hú Dié replied. "We should hurry."

I struggled for traction over the gelatinous frying oil that coated the pavement. I felt like a hockey player without skates. Jake stumbled beside me, and Phoenix grabbed his arm, steadying him.

An engine started, and we ducked behind a Dumpster. Brake lights flickered; we could make out a plain white panel van.

The vehicle didn't have side windows, but there were two glass rear windows reinforced with metal mesh. A light was on inside the van, and an Asian guy with skinny tattooed arms was struggling to lift something. He shifted out of view, and Peter's head flopped by the windows for a split second. He was unconscious and being pulled out of his wheelchair.

"Peter!" I shouted, and we sprinted after the van.

The light clicked off, the driver gunned the engine, and the van peeled onto the street. By the time we reached the end of the alley, the van was already picking up speed, and even though the traffic was heavy, it was immediately obvious that we wouldn't catch the van on foot. A motorcycle zoomed past, riding *between* two lanes of slower traffic. It gave me an idea.

"Guys!" I shouted. "The bikes! We can split lanes here!"

"Good thinking!" Hú Dié said.

"Jake," I said, "keep an eye on that van. Try to get the license plate number. We'll get your gear."

"Ten-four," Jake said.

Phoenix, Hú Dié, and I ran back to Peter's van. I saw the security bar clamped down on the bike frames, and I frowned. "I forgot about the lock. Peter has the key."

"Locks are like laws," Hú Dié said. "Eventually, somebody is going to break them."

She grabbed the rack with both hands and placed one foot on the bumper. She twisted her torso powerfully to one side, tearing the hitch-mounted rack free with a hair-raising *screech*.

"Locks are like laws, huh?" Phoenix said.

"Shut up, Phoenix," Hú Dié replied. "Help me break this bar off. Ryan, watch out for trouble."

No trouble came. Hú Dié and Phoenix had the security bar off in seconds. She was as skilled at taking things apart as she was at putting them together.

"Jake!" Hú Dié shouted. "Come on!"

He reached us quickly, looking excited. "Traffic is barely moving. I think we can catch them!" We jumped onto our bikes.

Pedaling was awkward at first because I wasn't wearing riding shoes with clips. My feet kept slipping off of the pedal shafts, but I soon got the hang of it.

I picked a line between two lanes of stop-and-go traffic and began to hammer forward. The others followed me in our tightest peloton yet. I could just make out the panel van in the glare of the taillights ahead.

Car horns began to honk, and Jake yelled out, "If you're jealous, go buy yourself a bike!"

The car exhaust was thick around us, and it made me a little light-headed. I was wearing cargo shorts, and warm, toxic air breezed over my skin each time I passed a muffler pipe pointed in my direction. I felt the rumble of trucks in my chest, and the whine of sports car engines buzzed in my ears as impatient drivers revved their vehicles when we blew past.

One idiot swerved in front of me, but I slowed and made it around him, as did Jake and then Phoenix.

Hú Dié, however, was last in our peloton. I glanced back to see the idiot swerve farther before stopping just a couple of feet from an idling car in the next lane. Hú Dié slowed to a crawl and rose out of her seat on one leg. She wouldn't make it through the slot with both legs astride her bike. She cocked her free leg up and back over her seat and wove through the slot, her free pedal shaft scratching a gouge in the idiot's chrome bumper. I turned my attention back to the road and smiled as the idiot started to shout behind us.

Hú Dié caught up with us, and we began to pick up speed.

"Sick moves, girl!" Jake shouted.

"That is how we do it back in Kaifeng!" Hú Dié shouted back.

We hurried on.

We were only four or five cars behind the white van when traffic began to open up. The van and all the vehicles around us started to accelerate.

So did I.

I felt a surge of energy burst forth from my *dan tien,* and I let my legs rip. I rode like a maniac for at least half a mile before glancing down at the electronic display attached to my handlebars. It was difficult to read with all of the headlights zipping past, but I soon made it out: thirty-eight miles per hour.

Even though I was flying, I was no longer keeping pace with traffic, and it was getting downright dangerous. I glanced back to find that the others were barely visible behind me. One of them signaled for me to slow.

I tapped my brakes and watched in disappointment as the white van began to pull away into the night. I slowed further, and my muscles began to tighten, including my *dan tien.* The van was very far ahead now, and I was about to give up hope, when in the distance it turned onto a side street.

I glanced around and noticed that the sidewalks here

were clear of people. Between gaps in the buildings, I saw lights glistening off of San Francisco Bay and realized we must be in an industrial district near the wharf.

There was a break in traffic, and I cut across to the sidewalk. I continued on at a moderate pace as the others cut over and joined me. My lungs were on fire and my muscles continued to cramp, but I wasn't about to quit.

"I don't know how much longer I can keep this up," Phoenix huffed.

"Me either," I said, struggling to catch my own breath. "But Peter needs us. The van turned down this street. Let's keep going."

I turned and saw that, mercifully, it was a long downhill run all the way to the waterfront. Brake lights flashed at the very end of the street, and I made out the white panel van turning left.

We coasted downhill, and my speedometer began to climb:

Forty miles per hour . . .

Forty-five miles per hour . . .

Even though I was exhausted and angry and my body was cramping terribly, I'd never felt such an exhilarating rush in my life.

I tickled my brakes as I neared the end of the street, and my arms and hands began to seize up. I guessed it was some kind of dragon bone fallout from having pushed so hard. I reached the end of the street and turned left with the others directly behind me. I continued to struggle for breath, but Phoenix and Hú Dié appeared to have gotten a second wind. They both shot past me, heading for the van, which had turned into the parking lot of a large waterfront building about a quarter mile up the road.

Jake pulled beside me.

"What's going on with you?" he huffed. "I've never seen anybody ride so fast like you did in that traffic!"

"I think it was the dragon bone," I huffed back. "It's like it wanted me to catch those guys and fight them or something."

"You might get your chance."

"We'll see. I'm cramping up tighter than a snare drum."

"Draft off of me," Jake said, and he pulled forward.

I locked onto his rear tire. As we neared, I saw that the building looked like some kind of warehouse. It was two stories tall and had large metal doors that looked like loading bays. Security flood lamps lighted up the entire perimeter.

The van stopped in front of the building, and Phoenix and Hú Dié raced up to it. Phoenix circled around to the driver's side, while Hú Dié approached the passenger side. They jumped off of their bikes and waited. No one got out.

The occupants must have seen us. What were they up to?

A full minute passed with no one exiting, and Hú Dié ran out of patience. She circled around to the back of the panel van, raised both arms, and slammed a hammer fist into each of the rear windows. They shattered into harmless safety glass pellets. The reinforcing metal mesh tore free of one window, and Hú Dié cocked an arm back again.

The barrel of a pistol poked out of the window.

"Gun!" she shouted.

Phoenix snaked around to the back of the van, hugging his body close to it. Then he let loose a front kick, and the pistol sailed into the night air. One of the van's rear doors burst open, and Phoenix grabbed somebody by the collar with both hands.

Jake and I reached the van as Phoenix yanked a skinny Asian man out of the vehicle. The guy had panthers tattooed up and down his arms. He tried to scramble to his feet, but Phoenix dropped a wicked elbow into the side of his head.

He folded like a wet sock.

A pair of huge, hairy hands shot out of the van, locking around Phoenix's neck. Phoenix cried out, but his shout was cut short, along with his air supply. He tried to push himself away, but his attacker's grip was too strong. Harsh light from the security flood lamps lit up burly forearms covered with silverback gorilla tattoos.

As I leaped off my bike, Hú Dié wailed like a banshee and jumped up, grabbing the top of the van's rear door frame. She tucked her legs into her chest before thrusting them into the van's interior. Phoenix was jerked powerfully backward, his body colliding with the van's closed door, before his attacker's grip released.

Someone unleashed a primal growl inside the van as Hú Dié swung back out into the parking lot. I grabbed Phoenix and dragged him away from the vehicle. He clambered to his feet, and I turned to see Hú Dié drop into a low Horse Stance.

The other rear door flew open, and a mountain of a man

emerged from the back of the van. He was Asian, easily stood six and a half feet tall, and probably weighed three hundred pounds.

"Phoenix!" Hú Dié shouted without taking her eyes off of the giant. "Are you okay?"

"Yeah," he replied.

"Double Flying Tiger—your way?" Hú Dié said.

"Go!" Phoenix said, and he ran at the man.

Hú Dié leaped into the air toward the gorilla-guy's head, lashing out with her right leg, while Phoenix sank low as if preparing to jump. The man raised both arms, slamming one mighty fist into Hú Dié's leg while keeping the other close to his face to protect it from Phoenix's airborne attack.

But Phoenix *didn't* jump. Instead, he drove both his fists up under the man's rib cage. Air rushed out of the giant's lungs with hurricane force and he buckled forward, knocking Phoenix out of the way, as Hú Dié crashed to the ground to one side.

I stepped up to the guy and dropped into a Horse Stance. My hands had cramped into rough approximations of tiger-claw fists, so I pulled both hands in to the sides of my chest like Hú Dié had taught me; then I thrust them forward with every ounce of strength I had left.

I roared like a lion, and the heels of my palms crashed into the bottom of the giant man's lowered chin. I felt a tremor run up my arms, and his head rocked back as if he'd been smacked with a club. His eyed rolled white, and he collapsed under his own enormous bulk.

Hú Dié sprang to her feet and looked at me in amazement. Phoenix had the same look on his face.

The van's driver's-side door opened, and Lin Tan stepped out. He held a gun. "Very impressive, Ryan," he said. "DaXing—*Gorilla*—is a former kung fu champion. Too bad kung fu is no match for bullets."

A door from the warehouse opened, and I heard muffled clapping. A slender Asian man in his sixties stepped into the parking lot. He was wearing a long-sleeved shirt and black leather gloves. Two younger Caucasian guys followed him, each carrying a shotgun. They stopped beside Lin Tan.

The older man stopped clapping.

"Excellent kung fu!" he said. "I haven't seen moves like that in generations. Your sequences were so . . . improvised. I enjoyed that immensely."

"Who are you?" I asked, though I already knew the answer. The gloves gave it away.

The man bowed slightly. "I am DuSow. Welcome. You must be the Mystery Teen Team, though you appear to be missing a member."

I looked around, confused. DuSow was right. I saw Phoenix and Hú Dié, but there was no sign of Jake.

18

"I didn't notice one of the kids sneak off," Lin Tan said.

"I did," DuSow said. "He rode away, then circled back. He's behind the warehouse. He submerged his bike and crawled beneath one of the docks. Very clever. Too bad he didn't consider security cameras. SaYui went to collect him."

I tried to straighten out of my Horse Stance but found that my leg muscles had locked up. My cramping was quickly growing worse.

DuSow said something in French, and one of the two cyclists with the shotguns headed toward the far corner of the building. Jake soon strode around it, followed by an Asian guy who also wore a cycling jersey and carried a gun. Jake was soaking wet. I thought the Asian guy's arms were dripping wet, too, but then I realized that it was actually tattoos. Sharks swirled and thrashed across his skin.

"SaYui," Phoenix muttered. *"Shark."*

Hú Dié nodded.

SaYui gave Jake a shove. "Go stand by your friends."

Jake walked over to me, his head low. He didn't say a word.

"Isn't this a pleasant surprise?" DuSow said. "I didn't plan to contact you until after the big race."

"What do you want from us?" Phoenix asked.

"Why, you're famous," DuSow said. "At least, in certain circles. I believe you can become famous in *all* circles. I am new to cycling, but it appears to be growing in popularity by leaps and bounds. I pride myself in being on the leading edge of new trends. You are going to ride on the team I am establishing. We are going to make a lot of money together."

"We are not going to ride for you!" Hú Dié said.

"That's right," Phoenix said. "Things didn't go so well for the last guy who tried to make me ride for him."

DuSow just laughed.

A gust of wind blew from DuSow's direction toward me, and I caught the scent of heavy cologne intermixed with a hint of dragon bone. My *dan tien* began to vibrate, and the rest of my body seized. I fell to the ground, my body compressing itself into a tight ball.

"Ryan!" Hú Dié said.

"Don't move," Lin Tan warned. "The same goes for you, Phoenix."

Lin Tan, SaYui, and the two guys with shotguns all aimed their weapons at Phoenix and Hú Dié as DuSow approached me. He bent down and inhaled deeply.

"Interesting," he said. "You looked like you might be

experiencing dragon bone complications. You are Ryan, correct? Dr. V's nephew?"

I didn't answer.

"That's him," Lin Tan said. "It looks like he could use another dose. I bet he's trying to wean himself from it."

"In all my years taking the substance," DuSow said, "I've never witnessed anyone attempt that. I'll have the doctor examine him. We may learn something."

There was a thump inside the van, and Peter nearly tumbled out of the back. He was so groggy, he could hardly lift his head.

"Leave . . . Ryan . . . alone," Peter mumbled.

DuSow looked at Lin Tan. "How much sedative did you give him?"

"Double the normal dose," Lin Tan replied, "like the doctor suggested."

"That man must have the constitution of an ox," DuSow said. "I'll take care of him."

DuSow removed his left glove and walked over to the van. I saw that the back of his hand was tattooed with images of lumpy-skinned toads.

"Don't touch him!" I grunted. "I have some dragon bone. I'll give it to you if you promise not to hurt Peter."

"Hurt him?" DuSow said. "My dear boy, I plan to heal him."

DuSow laid his bare hand on Peter's wobbly neck, and Peter went limp.

"No!" Hú Dié shouted.

DuSow looked to be amused. He turned to Hú Dié.

"Am I to understand that you know who I am, young lady? You seem frightened by my unique . . . skills."

"I have no idea who you are," Hú Dié lied. "I do know about Poison Hand kung fu, though. I know what those toads represent. Is he going to die?"

"Heavens, no," DuSow said. "As I said, my skills are unique. When most people think of Poison Hand kung fu, they think of this—"

He removed his other glove, uncovering what looked like a horror movie prop. His right hand was black and scaly, covered from wrist to fingertips with what looked like dry rot. I'd seen pictures of unwrapped mummy hands that were in better condition.

Hú Dié gasped.

"Let me show you something," DuSow said. He headed to the back of the van, where the unconscious DaXing and the guy with the panther tattoos lay. He knelt beside panther guy. "This man has disappointed me. I do not like to be disappointed."

With his right hand, DuSow gripped the man's throat. The man's eyelids flew open, and his body began to convulse and shudder. The skin of his neck turned as black as DuSow's hand, and I watched in horror as the discoloration spread all the way up to the man's ears. Soon the man's eyes closed again, and he stopped shuddering. His swollen tongue lolled out of his mouth.

DuSow released the man and turned to us. He raised both awful hands. "Left hand, good night. Right hand, goodbye."

Phoenix's shoulders slumped, and Jake turned away. Hú Dié's eyes burned with rage, but she kept them locked on to the ground.

DuSow put his gloves back on. "I would be greatly disappointed if the four of you did not join my team. I have read such interesting things about you on the Internet, and of course Lin Tan has told me plenty as well. You wouldn't want to disappoint me, would you?"

"No," Phoenix, Hú Dié, Jake, and I answered.

"Very good," DuSow said. "Now let me show you one more kung fu trick." He knelt next to DaXing.

"Please, don't," Hú Dié said.

DuSow ignored her. He grabbed the back of DaXing's huge neck with both gloved hands. I expected to hear bones crunch and vertebrae pop. Instead, DuSow began to work his fingers across the base of DaXing's skull as if he were kneading bread. A moment later, DaXing opened his eyes and sat up.

DuSow looked down at the gigantic man. "Get out of my sight. Take your failure of a friend with you and dispose of his body. I suggest the kiln. Disappoint me again and . . . well, you know."

DaXing nodded and stood. He lifted his dead friend into his arms and carried him into the warehouse.

"SaYui . . . Lucas . . . Philippe," DuSow said to the gun-toting guards. "Let me introduce you to your new teammates. This is Ryan, Phoenix, Jake, and Hú Dié."

The men scowled at us, and we scowled back.

"Lovely," DuSow said. "I am glad we are starting off on the right foot. Lucas and Philippe, escort Phoenix, Jake, and

Hú Dié to the research center. SaYui and I will bring Ryan, as it appears he is currently incapacitated."

"What about him?" Lin Tan asked, pointing at Peter.

"Throw him into his wheelchair and lock him in the stronghold. I don't want to take any chances. These teens are dangerous enough without their coach."

SaYui carried me, still curled into a ball, my muscles frozen stiff. Entering the warehouse, we passed through an office space. A large sign attached to the side wall read:

Tree Frog Imports
Beijing, China/San Francisco, USA

The company logo was a colorful frog with an arrow-shaped head—a poison dart frog.

Lucas gestured with his shotgun toward a closed door, and Philippe went through it, followed by Phoenix, Jake, and Hú Dié. DuSow went next, then finally SaYui and me. We wove through a series of corridors, and the air got progressively more stale and tinged with animal smells. It reminded me of a zoo.

Someone unlocked and opened a door, and a wave of foul odor made us all choke.

DuSow cleared his throat. "Doctor! Are you in here?"

"Sir?" replied a meek voice with a Chinese accent.

"Open the loading bay door!" DuSow ordered. "Air this place out."

"Yes, sir."

I heard a motor begin to whir as we entered an enormous research space. Across from us, a large door rose and rolled up overhead, but it did little to dissipate the smell.

I could see hundreds of small cages stacked on the filthy concrete floor. Each cage contained dozens of white mice. It looked—and smelled—like the overloaded cages hadn't been cleaned in months. My uncle had kept mice in his lab in Belgium, but they had been housed much differently, and they didn't stink like this.

The rest of this space couldn't be more different from my uncle's labs, either. Both his Belgium and Texas labs were state-of-the art and spotless. Whenever he tested me at either of them, it was like visiting a hospital. This place would have made Dr. Frankenstein cringe.

Open shelves lined the room, containing stacks of dusty, dried items. I could make out a stack of large rat skins, complete with fat, hairless tails. Another pile was bats, their paper-thin wings extended as if in flight. I also saw severed paws from numerous animals, including endangered species like polar bears and tigers.

I saw Hú Dié catch a glimpse of the paws, and her eyes went cold. Phoenix gripped her arm, anchoring her to his side so that she wouldn't take a swing at anybody. Lucas and Philippe ordered them to stand against a wall.

Phoenix, Hú Dié, and Jake stopped beside a huge pile of

rocks. Partial skeletons protruded from solid rock. Some of the bones looked longer than an elephant's leg, and I caught a glimpse of one jawbone that seemed much larger than an orca's. I was no paleontologist, but I would have bet my bank account that they were dinosaur fossils.

Next to the bones was a vacuum chamber like my uncle had. Elaborate pipework connected it to a larger network of pipes overhead.

The lights flickered for a second, and a loud fan began to rumble on the roof.

"Doctor?" DuSow said.

"That's just the kiln's exhaust fan," the doctor explained. "Someone must have turned it on in the next room."

SaYui laid me on a stained table that was made of chipped particleboard. I tried not to think about what the stains were, or where they might have come from.

"SaYui," DuSow said, "go retrieve the bikes. Bring them in here."

"Yes, sir," SaYui said, and he left through the loading bay door.

From my new position, I could see the far corner of the room opposite my friends. I saw three matching road bikes beside a rack that contained helmets, shoes, and other gear that also matched.

"Join us, Doctor," DuSow said. "I have a new patient for you to examine."

The doctor came over, and I got my first look at him. He was an old Chinese man with white hair. He wore a dirty lab coat, and he stared at me through thick-lensed glasses.

His narrow eyes appeared huge and reptilian behind the magnification. He pushed his large, flat nose an inch from my cheek and inhaled.

"Dragon bone?" the doctor asked.

"Yes," DuSow said.

The doctor began to probe my rigid muscles with his thin, yellow-nailed fingers. "Withdrawal?"

"I believe so," DuSow said. "He said that he possessed some. Let's see if he has it with him now."

DuSow opened one of my cargo shorts' large pockets and removed my cell phone and wallet. He flipped through my wallet, then put it back into my pocket.

"I am many things," DuSow said, "but a common thief is not one of them."

He placed my phone on a shelf beside a pile of dried pig ears and checked my other cargo pocket. He removed my vial of dragon bone and handed it to the doctor. The doctor opened the vial and smelled the contents.

The doctor smiled, showing brown, crooked teeth. "It's dragon bone. Very high quality. Where did it come from?"

"The same place as Lin Tan's," DuSow said.

"Did someone call me?"

Lin Tan entered the loading bay door with SaYui. They were pushing our bikes, which they leaned against a cluster of mice cages.

SaYui took up a position beside Lucas and Philippe, while Lin Tan walked over to DuSow.

"The coach is in the stronghold," Lin Tan said. "What's next?"

"I was about to suggest that the doctor give Ryan a dose of dragon bone," DuSow replied. "I'd like to see if he snaps out of this condition."

"No," I said through clenched teeth. "No more dragon bone."

"You're in no position to argue," DuSow said. "Doctor, give him the team's usual dosage."

The doctor placed my vial of dragon bone on the shelf next to my phone and pulled a larger container from another shelf. I watched, helpless, as the doctor scooped four times my normal amount into a test tube. The substance was light gray, like my dragon bone.

"That's too much!" I said.

"Nonsense," the doctor replied. "Lin Tan has been taking this same amount for months. So have SaYui, Lucas, and Philippe, though theirs is my manufactured version. My research indicates that this is the optimum quantity. Since you have been taking the pure version, that is what I am giving you."

He added a small amount of clear liquid to the test tube; then he stoppered it and shook it. Once the dragon bone had dissolved, he removed the stopper and stepped up to me.

"Please!" I begged. "Don't!" I felt my *dan tien* begin to quiver expectantly, and I wished I could punch myself in the stomach to make it stop.

My mind began to race. "Acupuncture!" I said. "Try that instead. It worked before."

"Acupuncture?" DuSow said. "Hmmm. I would never have considered that. I don't have any experience with it, though. Do you, Doctor?"

The doctor shook his head. "Only on mice."

"Proceed, then," DuSow said. "Open wide, Ryan."

"No!" I shouted.

I heard Phoenix, Hú Dié, and Jake begin to shuffle their feet uncomfortably, and I glanced over to see Lucas, Philippe, and SaYui aiming their guns at them. I knew my friends would have helped me if they could.

The doctor pinched my nose closed and pressed the vial to my lips. I kept my mouth closed and held my breath as long as I could, but it was pointless. The instant I opened my mouth to take a breath, the doctor poured the dissolved dragon bone in. With surprising strength, he slammed my jaw closed. I gagged and choked, reflexively swallowing several times before the doctor released his grip on me.

I felt white fire rush from my *dan tien* to every one of my extremities. My body jolted, then went limp.

No one spoke for a moment.

Finally, the doctor asked, "Can you move?"

"I . . . don't know," I said.

My arms and legs felt like spaghetti. My head was a bowling ball at the end of a string. I willed one of my fingers to move, and, surprisingly, it obeyed.

"Very good," the doctor said. "You'll be good as new in a few minutes."

The doctor turned out to be right. I willed my other fingers to move, and then my toes. They all worked fine. Everything came back online like a computer rebooting.

I sat up and felt incredible. My head was clear for the first time in weeks, and my senses were keener than ever. My muscles throbbed expectantly, as if ready for some kind of action. If I were to race at that very moment, I had no doubt that I would beat anyone—including Phoenix in a sprint.

And I hated it.

DuSow grinned. "Feels good, doesn't it?"

"No," I said. "It feels . . . unnatural."

"You'll come to love it," DuSow said, "just like everyone else."

I glanced at Lucas, Philippe, and SaYui. "But they're going to *die*."

"Not necessarily," DuSow said. "The doctor believes he has found a way to filter out most of the dragon bone impurities. We will see soon enough if his technique works. These men know the risks."

The doctor glanced at Phoenix, Jake, and Hú Dié. "New test subjects?"

I shoved the old man. "You are *not* going to give this stuff to my friends!"

DuSow grabbed my upper arms, gripping me like a vice. His gloved fingers sank into my biceps, hitting some sort of pressure points. Pain shot all the way up to my armpits.

"I strongly suggest you keep your hands to yourself," DuSow said.

I nodded, and DuSow's grip relaxed, stopping the pain. However, his hands remained on my upper arms.

"I will not be administering dragon bone to teenagers," DuSow said. "For what it's worth, I despise the fact that your uncle gave some to you."

"You knew him?" I asked.

"Indirectly," DuSow said. "I sold fossils to Lin Tan, who

in turn sold them to your uncle. It may have been my best business transaction in decades. His initial queries, coupled with my own dragon bone use and my questions concerning techniques and equipment, inspired me to manufacture the substance myself. Our research has revealed a potential use for dragon bone beyond your uncle's sole focus of performance enhancement and the legendary use for lengthening one's life expectancy."

"Peter," I said.

"Yes, Peter. Imagine the headlines when the world-famous para-cyclist walks again. I could have picked any number of people in his condition, but a celebrity endorsement is so much better. There are tens of millions of people like Peter, and many will pay a fortune to be able to walk once more. True, they may not be able to run marathons or race bicycles because of concerns about overexertion, but it's a worthy trade-off."

"Don't give it to Peter," I said. "I don't think he'd want it."

"He doesn't," Lin Tan said. "When I offered it to him in that alley, he said that he'd rather drink gasoline and swallow a match."

"He'll thank us for it later," DuSow said.

"No!" I felt my face turn red with rage. I glared at DuSow, and Lin Tan raised his pistol to my forehead.

"Put the gun down," DuSow said. "The boy isn't going to do anything. Are you?"

I ground my teeth and shook my head. I thought about trying one of my new kung fu moves, but there were too many guns in the room. Also, DuSow's hands were too close for comfort.

"Did you give Peter dragon bone from your supply?" DuSow asked Lin Tan.

"Of course not," Lin Tan said. "I gave him some of the doctor's manufactured version."

"In that case," the doctor said, "I don't expect we'll see any results for at least a couple days."

The lights flickered again, and DuSow glanced at the doctor. The doctor shrugged.

In the darkness beyond the open loading bay door, I thought I heard a faint clicking on the pavement.

"Do you hear that?" DuSow asked.

"Yeah," Lin Tan said. "I'll go check it out."

He was halfway to the door when all the lights cut out and the room went black.

In the sudden darkness, someone shouted, "Run!"

It was Jake's voice.

A bright light flashed on just outside the open door, and a powerful beam played around the room. The beam stopped on Lin Tan, who froze like a deer in headlights.

CRACK! CRACK!

Two quick shots echoed through the research center, Lin Tan's body jolting with each one. He fell to the ground.

I stared at the light source and saw that it was mounted to a rifle.

Bo held the rifle.

Beside him stood Bones.

BOOM! One of the shotguns fired, and Bo cried out. He flipped off the light, and I heard Bones attack. In the darkness, someone began to scream in French.

People started to scramble, and I reached for the shelves

beside me. I found my phone and turned on the display just long enough to locate my dragon bone vial, then pocketed both items.

Bo's light flicked on again, and the beam passed over Phoenix and Jake, who were running toward the loading bay door. The beam settled on SaYui, who was scanning the room with his pistol.

The muzzle of Bo's rifle flashed.

CRACK!

SaYui went down.

The beam shifted over to Bones, who was on top of Lucas. One of Lucas's arms was between Bones's jaws. I saw a glint of metal, and Bo shifted the beam beyond Bones a few feet. Philippe was shouldering his shotgun.

SMACK!

Hú Dié's fist appeared out of the darkness, knocking Philippe out cold. Bones glared at Hú Dié, but the dog didn't release its grip on the struggling Lucas. Hú Dié kicked Lucas's head, putting him to sleep, but Bones still didn't let go.

I headed for the loading bay door and heard a loud click near me.

"Bo!" I shouted. "Gun!"

The beam of light swung in my direction to illuminate the doctor fumbling with Lin Tan's pistol.

CRACK!

The doctor fell to the ground, dropping the pistol. I picked it up on the way past.

A door opened across the room, and Bo shined the light

toward it. DuSow was heading through the door we'd used to enter.

CRACK!

The door frame splintered from Bo's shot as DuSow disappeared back into the warehouse corridor.

"Damn," Bo said. He shined his light back on Lucas and said, "Bones! Release!"

Bones released the unconscious man's arm and trotted toward Bo. Beyond Bones, Hú Dié rounded up the two shotguns and SaYui's pistol.

I kept the doctor's pistol pointed in a safe direction and hurried to Bo's side. He was wearing a tool belt with a huge buckle that read TEXAS ELECTRIC. "Are you going into the warehouse after that guy?"

"Naw," Bo said. "That's DuSow. I'd rather climb into a rattlesnake nest than go after him. If he wants to come chase me back home on my turf, he's more than welcome to try. I got what I came for." He moved the beam until it rested on Lin Tan's still figure.

I shivered.

Hú Dié walked over to us. She held the two shotguns in the crook of one arm but gripped SaYui's pistol as if ready to use it. Bones growled but didn't attack.

"I think he appreciates what you done, Ms. Hú Dié," Bo said. "You don't have to worry about him no more."

Hú Dié shrugged and looked at Bo's leg. "Are you going to be okay?"

I noticed for the first time that Bo's leg was bleeding.

"I'll be fine," Bo said. "Good thing that Frenchman

didn't have very good aim. I hardly notice it. That's the leg Phoenix slammed in the car door." He grinned.

"Sorry," Phoenix said, hurrying over with Jake. "Kind of. What are you doing here?"

"Jake called me," Bo said.

"Huh?" I said. "How did he get your number?"

Jake grinned. "I remembered it! I was standing next to you when he gave you his number back at Point Lobos. I called him when you three were fighting DuSow's guys."

"*You're* the mutant, Jake," I said. "Nobody else could have remembered that."

Jake chuckled.

"You're lucky I was close by," Bo said. "I had followed you all from Peter's to Chinatown."

"Peter!" I said. "We have to find him. They said he was in the stronghold."

"Uh-oh," Bo said, shaking his head. "He's probably on that boat that left."

"What boat?"

Bo pointed toward the bay. "As I was coming up, I noticed a boat pulling out. The name on the back was *The Strong Hold*."

"I am sorry, Ryan," Hú Dié said, "but we need to leave. DuSow is still here."

"She's right," Bo said. "But I don't have room for you all plus Bones in my truck. The bed is full."

"No sweat," Jake said. "We'll ride."

"Your bike is at the bottom of the bay," Phoenix said.

"I'll borrow one," Jake said. "Remember, these guys race." He pointed to a flashlight clipped to Bo's belt, and Bo

THE FIVE ANCESTORS OUT OF THE ASHES

handed it to him. Jake disappeared into the back corner of the room, behind the maze of shelves.

I glanced at the pistol in my hand. "I need to get rid of this."

"I have a few to get rid of, too," Hú Dié said. "Come on."

We threw the guns into the bay and retrieved our bikes with the aid of Bo's rifle-mounted light. Phoenix grabbed his bike, too.

Jake called out, "Hú Dié! Can you come help me?"

Hú Dié shook her head. "Pick out one road bike for him, and I become his personal mechanic."

She disappeared behind the shelves and soon came out with Jake. They were wearing helmets and Jake was pushing one of the three road bikes I'd seen earlier. Hú Dié tossed helmets to me and Phoenix.

"Nice knowing you—now get lost," Bo said, and he limped toward a line of moonlit trees with Bones at his side.

We raced around the building, onto the road. I half expected DuSow to come barreling after us in the van, but he didn't.

"Where to?" Phoenix shouted. "Hok's?"

"Yeah!" I shouted back. "But I'm not sure I remember the way."

"*I* remember!" Jake shouted. "Follow me!"

Jake got us to Chinatown faster than I thought possible. We climbed off our bikes at the Dragon Gate entrance and quickly pushed our way through the still-crowded streets.

"Nice work, Jake," I said.

Hú Dié nodded. "Yes. Your memory is amazing."

Phoenix patted him on the back. "Way to go, bro."

Jake beamed.

We reached Waverly Place, and I saw that the guys who'd been hanging out in front of Hok's a few hours ago were now gone. I heard a noise overhead and looked up to see her on the balcony.

"Dear me," she said. "Is something the matter?"

"Big-time," I said. "Can we come up?"

"Of course. Leave your bicycles in the entry. No one will tamper with them."

We hurried up the low, narrow staircase. She was waiting for us outside her door, and we ran inside.

"What's the hurry?" she asked.

"DuSow has taken Peter," I said. "He tried to keep us, too, but we escaped."

"Oh, my," Hok said. "Did he follow you?"

I shook my head. "I don't think so."

"Well done," Hok said. "Come into the kitchen and tell me the details."

The four of us sat at her kitchen table and filled her in as she stirred a small pot of liquid simmering on the stove. The longer she stirred, the hungrier I got. I was starving. We were supposed to have eaten a Chinatown dinner with Peter hours ago. She kept lifting the wooden spoon in the air to check the consistency of the liquid, and it was driving me crazy. It smelled delicious.

As soon as we'd finished getting Hok up to date, Jake asked, "Can I have some of whatever it is you're cooking? I'm starving."

"I'm sorry," Hok said. "I should have asked if you were

hungry when you first arrived. That is a traditional Chinese greeting, you know, *Chi le ma*—'Have you eaten yet?' It doesn't always mean that literally, but you'll hear it often around Chinatown."

"That's my kind of greeting!" Jake said. "What's cookin'?"

"Nothing for you, I'm afraid. This is medicine."

"That is the sweetest medicine I've ever smelled," I said.

Hok laughed. "Really? Do you want to know what is in here?"

"Maybe not," I said.

"I do!" Jake said.

Hok nodded. "Dried flying lizard. Very good for boosting one's metabolism."

"Yuck," Jake said. "Got anything else?"

"I have some things you might like in my refrigerator. Do you like *longan*—dragon eye fruit?"

"Yum!" Hú Dié said.

"I like it," Phoenix said.

"I don't know," Jake said. "I've kind of had it with dragon stuff."

"I hear that," I said.

Hú Dié nudged Jake in the side. "Hey, are you forgetting something?"

"What?" Jake said. "I—oh, yeah! I have something for *you*, Hok."

Jake unbuttoned one of the pockets of his cargo shorts and pulled out a small bottle that was stoppered with a cork. It appeared to contain several dozen tiny green curlicues, and there was a Chinese character written on it with gold paint. He set the bottle on the table, and Hok quickly snatched it up with a towel over her hand.

"Go to the sink, Jake!" she snapped. "Wash your hands immediately!"

Jake turned white as a ghost and leaped to his feet. He began to scrub his hands vigorously.

Hok wiped the bottle down and set it on the kitchen counter. She threw the towel into the garbage and turned to Jake. "Show me your hands," she said.

Jake pulled his dripping hands out of the sink and thrust them toward her. She looked them over without touching them; then she nodded. "You are fine. Dry your hands and sit back down."

Jake lowered his hands to wipe them on his shorts. "No!" Hok snapped. "Try not to put your hands anywhere near the pocket where you kept this bottle. As soon as you are able, dispose of those clothes. I doubt they have been contaminated, but you can never be too careful."

"What is that stuff?" I asked.

Hú Dié frowned. "Dragon tongue. Remember when Jake called me over in DuSow's research room? He did not want to ask me about the bikes. He saw bottles that all had different Chinese labels."

"I thought I remembered the Chinese character from Hok's recipe for the dragon bone antidote, but I wanted to be sure," Jake said.

"Bro," I said. "You truly are a mutant."

Jake shrugged. "Only trying to help."

Hok smiled. "And help, you did. It just so happens that

what is on the stove is a batch of the antidote. I was preparing everything short of the dragon tongue so I could reheat it and add the final ingredient if I ever managed to acquire some. You have saved me a lot of trouble. Thank you."

Jake grinned.

"Is it really that toxic?" Phoenix asked.

"Yes," Hok replied. "In fact, I am going to stay on this side of the room for a moment. Once I add the final ingredient, I do not want to risk any of you breathing in dust from the substance."

Hok stoppered her sink and filled it with water. She put on a pair of gloves and took a pair of tweezers out of a drawer. She gripped the dragon bone bottle with one hand and removed the cork stopper; then she pulled out a curlicue with the tweezers and dropped it into the small pot.

The simmering liquid suddenly became a rolling boil, and Hok hurriedly replaced the cork stopper. She tossed the tweezers and gloves into the water-filled sink and hurriedly washed her hands. Then she began to stir the pot with the wooden spoon she'd been using earlier. The boil soon settled back down to a simmer, and she turned off the stove.

"Done," she said. "It reacted just as the recipe said it would. Now all I need is someone to try it out on."

I cleared my throat. "Do you really think it will work?"

"I do not know," Hok said, "but you will not be the first to try it. It is far too dangerous. Someone else can be the guinea pig."

She picked up the bottle of dragon tongue, and we followed her into the room with all the wooden drawers. She opened one that wasn't labeled and carefully placed the bottle inside; then she closed the drawer.

Someone pounded on the door.

"Open up!" a voice demanded.

I recognized the voice. It was DuSow.

21

"We have to hide!" I said in a low voice.

"The balcony?" Phoenix whispered.

Hok shook her head. "No one is going anywhere. He will have seen your bicycles. He knows you are here. Even if you did manage to sneak out, he would find you.

"Coming!" Hok called out. She unlocked the door and opened it.

DuSow strolled in without a word, followed by DaXing, the huge guy with the gorilla tattoos. DaXing carried Lin Tan, whose entire chest was bandaged and splashed with red.

I couldn't believe Lin Tan was still alive. Then again, I shouldn't have been surprised. Dragon bone worked in mysterious ways.

Hú Dié looked as if she were about to rip DuSow's head off. "How did you find us?"

"Please," DuSow said. "I knew you'd been here before

you arrived at my warehouse. I received even more calls when you returned."

"What do you want?" Hok asked.

"I'll get right to the point," DuSow said. "I expect you to heal my associate, Lin Tan. He was shot twice in the chest. These children are responsible."

"Us!" I said. "We—"

Hok raised a hand to silence me. "I will handle this." She looked at Lin Tan's blood-soaked bandages. "Two bullets to the chest would kill most people."

"Are you going to heal him or not?" DuSow ask.

"Why me?"

"I can smell the dragon bone seeping out of your pores from five feet away, that's why."

Hok closed her eyes. "So Lin Tan is a dragon bone user?"

"You said it yourself, his wounds would have killed most people."

"And you want me to cure him?"

"Do you need me to explain it to you in Chinese?" DuSow asked, beginning to lose his cool. "Yes, cure him!"

Hok nodded. "Lay him on the floor."

DaXing laid Lin Tan down on Hok's hardwood floor, and Hok headed into the kitchen. She returned a moment later carrying a small Chinese teacup. I caught a whiff of its contents, and I tried to keep my expression neutral. It was the dragon bone antidote.

Hok set the teacup down on the floor beside Lin Tan.

"What is that?" DuSow asked as he squatted down and peered into the cup, sniffing. "It doesn't smell like tea."

"It is blood tonic. I just completed a batch. Would you like some?"

DuSow stood. "No. I know flying lizard when I smell it. It is supposed to be good for your metabolism, but I never touch the stuff."

"Suit yourself," Hok said. "It will make a world of difference for Lin Tan. I promise."

She first removed Lin Tan's bandages, examining his wounds. I turned away. I couldn't watch.

"It appears as though he is healing at a tremendous rate," Hok said. "He does not seem to be losing any more blood."

"I already knew that," DuSow said. "I just want to make sure he survives. He is important to my organization."

Hok replaced Lin Tan's bandages with fresh ones and cradled his head in one hand. She lifted the teacup with the other hand, gently raising it to Lin Tan's lips, and she poured the liquid into his mouth. He coughed and sputtered, then swallowed the entire mouthful.

Lin Tan's body began to ripple like a dying fish, slowly at first, then faster and faster. His heels banged against the wooden floor as his head jerked in Hok's hands.

"What's happening?" DuSow asked.

"I am curing him," Hok replied, "like you wanted."

"You call *that* curing?"

"His complications are great. The cure must be greater."

Lin Tan's undulations soon slackened, and his body curled up, tightening into a rigid ball exactly as mine had done earlier. He trembled once, then relaxed entirely.

"I've never seen anything quite like that in all my years," DuSow said. "Is he going to live?"

"I hope so," Hok said. "Take him with you and keep an eye on him. Do you have my telephone number?"

"I can get it if I need it," DuSow said.

"Call me if his condition worsens. Otherwise, tomorrow morning I will call you or whomever you select as his caregiver to follow up." She handed him a pencil and a pad of paper from a small desk. "Give me a number, please."

DuSow shoved the paper and pencil at DaXing. "You get the honors of playing nursemaid. Give the woman your cell phone number."

The giant scribbled down a number and handed the items back to Hok. She placed them on the desk.

"We'll be leaving now," DuSow said.

"Not yet," Hok said. "We have something to discuss."

"And that would be?"

"Ryan's cousin, Peter."

"I don't know what you're talking about."

Hok's eyes narrowed. "Do not disrespect me, DuSow. You know exactly what I am talking about. Everyone turns a blind eye to your activities, including me, but I will not look away from this one. I welcomed you into my home and I healed your associate. I am not asking for repayment; I am asking for a favor. Let Peter go."

DuSow waved his hand and turned his back to Hok. "I am done with you."

Hok grabbed DuSow by the arm and said in a low voice, "You are an important person here in Chinatown,

DuSow. So am I. Do not test me. What are your plans for Peter?"

DuSow grinned. "Strong words from a strong woman. I can appreciate that. How about we make a deal? I am interested to see these teens race as planned next week in order to keep the race's attention level high. I have received word that cycling journalists from several countries will be there, including China, thanks to Hú Dié and Phoenix's involvement. If all four teens race, I will let their coach go. If they do not race, or if they go to the authorities, Peter will never be seen again."

"Let Peter go now!" I blurted out.

DuSow shook his head. "No. My offer stands. Take it, or leave it."

Hok looked at me. "Do you agree to this deal?"

I felt my hands begin to shake. "Why would I?"

DuSow raised his gloved right hand and wiggled his fingers at me. "Here are five good reasons."

My blood ran cold and my face turned red. Hok put her hand on my shoulder. "Calm yourself, Ryan. I am afraid this is how business is done in Chinatown. I do not like it any more than you do, but DuSow holds all the cards."

"You should be grateful that I'm offering a deal at all," DuSow said.

I turned to Phoenix, Hú Dié, and Jake. "What do you guys think?"

"This isn't a deal," Phoenix said. "It's straight-up kidnapping. But I'll race if you want me to."

"I will race, too," Hú Dié said, "if that is what you wish."

"Heck yeah, bro," Jake said. "I'm looking forward to smoking those clowns."

I turned back to DuSow and glared at him. "We're in, but we're not racing for *you*. We're racing for Peter."

"Whatever motivates you," DuSow said. "See you at the race."

I woke late the next morning in Hok's guest bedroom with my mother's head hovering over mine. Hok stood beside her. I glanced at the clock and saw that it was past noon.

My mom kissed me on the cheek. "Good morning, sunshine. How are you?"

I felt my face begin to flush with embarrassment. Fortunately, Phoenix, Hú Dié, and Jake weren't there to hear her. I saw that Hú Dié had made her bed, and the guys had neatly rolled up the mats they'd slept on.

"I'm exhausted," I said, "and please don't call me that."

"Sorry, dear," she said, patting me on the head like a puppy.

I grimaced.

Hok smiled. "Your mother cares deeply for you, Ryan. You are a lucky young man."

"I know," I said, sitting up. "Thanks for coming to help us train, Mom."

"I wouldn't miss it for the world," she said. "Hok told me about your adventures yesterday when she picked me up at the airport. I am very upset about Peter, and it took Hok a solid hour to calm me down. But as she convinced me, it is beyond our control. We must focus on the things that are within our grasp, like winning that race."

I shook my head. "I don't know. I'm really upset about Peter, too, and it's not like we're going to win. I checked the roster last night. More teams were invited to ride. Some of the guys are category *two* racers."

"You certainly aren't going to win with an attitude like that!" my mother snapped. "Don't let thoughts about Peter distract you from your goal. You can think about him after the race. I bet he wants you to win even more than you."

"But we're not even category five racers and—"

"The reason you're not cat five is that you've never participated in a sanctioned road race," my mother said. "Categories and rankings mean nothing in this event. It isn't even sanctioned. It's a publicity stunt. However, it's shaping up to be an important publicity stunt. There are already rumors of it becoming a full-blown event next year. Doing well next week could set the stage for big things to happen to the top finishers. Your father and Peter were in a position like this once, you know."

"They were?"

"Yes. The race in which Peter wrecked was for all the marbles, so to speak."

I frowned. "Oh."

"Why the sad face? What happened happened. Good things did come out of that."

"Like what?"

"You, for one."

"Huh?"

"After Peter crashed, your father hung up his helmet. He decided to stop racing and focus on having a family. If he'd have continued riding, you wouldn't be here."

"Oh," I said. "But Peter—"

"Peter accepts the hand life dealt him. You should, too."

"Your mother is right," Hok said.

"I guess," I said. "I'm still worried about him, though."

"Me too," my mother said, "but we'll see him soon enough."

"Are we going to stay at his house?"

"Yes. The others tell me there is a hidden house key?"

"Yeah."

"Perfect. I've reserved a rental van with a bike rack. We'll be leaving as soon as you and the others finish lunch. They're in the kitchen right now. You should join them."

"I will. What about Peter's van?"

"It's best to leave it where it is parked. Eventually, the police will tow it away. Peter can collect it next week. I'll help him pay the fine if he wishes. If that DuSow character doesn't keep his word, the abandoned vehicle will be important evidence in a police investigation."

I sighed. "Maybe we should just go to the police now."

"I don't think so," my mother said. "I've been on the phone with Phoenix's grandfather, and he is convinced that we should let things play out 'like the old days,' as he said. He's been around a very long time, and he seems to know a lot about criminals. He thinks going to the police is a particularly bad idea because DuSow likely has informants within the force. I trust his judgment."

"Phoenix's grandfather is indeed intelligent," Hok said, "and he is correct about informants."

"If you say so," I said. "Did you hear anything more about Lin Tan?"

"I called DaXing earlier this morning," Hok replied. "I ended up speaking directly with Lin Tan. He is doing well, and his wounds have stopped their accelerated healing."

"The antidote?" I said. "It worked? Does he know what you did?"

"It is very possible that it worked. His reaction last night led me to believe so. I convinced him this morning that he needs to stop taking dragon bone in order to heal properly. He hinted that he no longer wanted to consume it, anyway. I told him that he might be done with the substance for good—that he had 'bled it out' of his system. He seemed pleased with that. I do not think he will be taking it anymore."

I glanced down at my *dan tien*.

"Don't even think about it," my mother said. "Hok told me all about the antidote and the poison in it. Who knows what kind of complications might arise from the substance. You aren't going to be taking it anytime soon."

"But Lin Tan is fine," I said.

"We don't know that," Hok said. "You should at least wait awhile and see what happens to him before considering the antidote."

"How much more do you have?" I asked.

"Enough for five doses, so put it out of your mind. We

will return to Uncle Tí's schedule for weaning you from the substance. If the large dose you were given yesterday has thrown things off, we will adjust accordingly. Your mother and I have already discussed it."

I looked at my mother.

She nodded.

"All right," I said.

"Good!" my mom said. "Let's get moving, sunshine. I'm anxious to see you guys ride." She winked.

I rolled my eyes and got out of bed.

I joined the others in the kitchen and ate lunch while my mom picked up the van. Then we loaded the bikes and hit the road. Instead of going directly to Peter's, my mom drove us to the race location, which wasn't too far from Chinatown. The short, mile-long race route was posted online, and my mom had printed out a copy. We followed the route loop three times before we were satisfied. The race organizers seemed to have gone out of their way to select as many hills as possible. A section of the hill we'd ridden last night was even included. It was going to be tough.

The route passed within blocks of DuSow's warehouse, and though we couldn't see the warehouse from the route, we could see his docks from one of the taller hills. There was no sign of *The Strong Hold*.

Finally, we headed south. As we rolled into Peter's driveway, Ms. Bettis was out walking her dog, and she waved to us. I'd nearly forgotten about her and my crashing Peter's handcycle. It seemed like months ago, but it had been less than two weeks. Crazy.

I retrieved Peter's spare key from its hiding place, and

we put the bikes in the garage. This included the bike Jake had "borrowed" from DuSow. For some reason, DuSow hadn't taken it back when he and his goons left Hok's, so we brought it with us. My mom asked Jake if he wanted her to buy him a new one, but he said, "No way!" He thought the bike would give him good mojo when racing against DuSow's team. I hoped he was right.

My mom *had* purchased, however, handlebar-mounted bike lights for us. She got them back in Indiana, and she brought them with her on the flight. She also brought small gear bags to hang beneath our bike seats so that we could carry a cell phone and identification in case we ever got into a wreck. We unloaded these things, as well, and headed into the house.

The first thing we did once we were inside was rock-paper-scissors to take showers. I got to go first. It took me ten minutes to wash all the San Francisco road funk out of my hair. Vented helmets were great for airflow, but lousy for keeping bits of asphalt, dirt, and flying insects out of your scalp. The hot shower felt awesome.

After I'd finished, I sat down with my mom and my computer tablet to try to find places for us to train at night.

"We need a well-lit subdivision for the first few nights," my mom said, "then progressively darker ones to mimic the race route conditions you'll experience."

I used Internet map software to identify possible nearby locations, and then daytime satellite images to help determine which subdivisions had streetlights and which didn't. However, as I'd seen last night in San Francisco, just because a street had lights didn't mean they worked, so we'd have to do a little reconnaissance.

Which is exactly what we did.

After everyone was cleaned up, we grabbed some food at a local restaurant and headed out. We drove for hours first in daylight, then darkness. We found a few suitable subdivisions, a couple of which had hills. None of us were looking forward to riding those hills, but we knew we had to in order to simulate the race conditions.

We discussed race strategy as we drove, and my mom explained the importance of our working together.

"Criteriums are solo races," she said, "but a rider can increase his or her odds of winning dramatically by working with others."

"Yeah," I said, "Peter told us that. But is it legal?"

"It's frowned upon by certain crit riders, but it isn't against the rules. The primary advantage to forming your own pack is protection. Criteriums are quite physical. Riders jostle for position the entire time, with elbows and knees flying freely. Pack members can protect themselves better by forming walls or wedges to keep the other riders away, depending on the situation."

"What about equipment?" Hú Dié asked. "I modified my bike before I raced in a criterium, and it helped a lot."

"You won't be able to do that," my mom said. "Serious crit racers use custom bikes with a shorter wheelbase to help them steer quicker and control the bike better overall. They're more cramped and uncomfortable to ride than a regular road bike, but the race is only an hour, so the discomfort is worth it. Unfortunately, we don't have the time to find someone to chop up your bikes and put them back together in time for the race."

"I can do it," Hú Dié said.

My mom shook her head. "I know you build bicycles and Peter has a shop right here, but besides cutting sections out of the frames and welding them back together, you'd have to make other modifications. It's complicated."

"It's not that bad," Hú Dié said. "I'd just have to cut down everyone's cranks so that our toes wouldn't bump the front tires on sharp turns. I've done it a bunch of times for cyclocross racers. It worked great. Let me give it a try. I'll do my bike first and show you."

"She's very good," Phoenix said. "Fast, too. If she says she can do it, she means it."

"I give in," my mom said. "I'll let you modify yours, Hú Dié, and we'll see how long it takes you and how well it performs."

We got back to Peter's, and Hú Dié went straight to the garage while the rest of us went to bed. I wasn't at all surprised when I woke the next morning to find that Hú Dié had been up all night, modifying her bike. It worked perfectly, and my mom was blown away. She gave Hú Dié the green light to do the same thing to ours. Hú Dié went to sleep, asking to be woken up a few hours before we'd have to go train in the dark.

We fell into a routine from that point on, following Hú Dié's lead of sleeping most of the day and staying up most of the night. My mom thought it would help us have more energy for the nighttime race, and she was right.

· · ·

When race day came, we felt great. We'd trained as hard as we could, and since my mom's experience with bicycles came from my dad and Peter, her coaching drills were very similar to Peter's. We'd polished the skills we'd already been working on, only this time in the dark, and we continued to gel as a team, learning how far each of us could push before burning out. Jake blew us all away with the progress he'd made, and I didn't have any significant dragon bone issues after going back to the schedule Uncle Tí had made for me. We were ready to race.

Or so I thought. I began to have second thoughts once we arrived at the starting line.

Our opponents were animals. I'd never felt intimidated when racing before, even when I'd trained with members of my uncle's cyclocross team. However, these guys were different, like my mom said they would be. They were all intensely focused, and many were jacked up to the size of NFL running backs. Their bodies had been forged for power and speed as opposed to endurance like most riders.

Hú Dié walked around with a big, goofy grin on her face, batting her eyes at just about every guy who passed. Jake and Phoenix, however, looked as worried as I was.

Worst of all, it was raining. Leave it to my luck for sunny California to be hit with showers the night of the big race. Hok had told me it rained in San Francisco more than southern California, but I hadn't paid it any mind.

I thought about her and frowned. She'd called earlier

to tell us that she wouldn't be attending the race. She said that she would only be a distraction for us, especially since DuSow was bound to be here. She didn't want to risk a confrontation.

The race was going to be broadcast live over an Internet feed, and Hok said that she was going to watch us that way. She was also going to record it so that, according to her, we could relive our victory again and again. Looking around me, I was pretty certain I'd never want to see that recording. We were going to get creamed.

My mom walked over to me. "How are you doing?"

"Nervous," I said. "These guys are going to ride all over us."

"You'll be fine."

"I don't think so. A lot of these guys are bigger than *me*."

"That's good. They can block the wind and rain for you, on the sides as well as in front."

"I'd rather not think about the rain."

"Why? Because of what happened to Peter?"

I nodded.

"I told you, forget about him until after the race."

Phoenix, Hú Dié, and Jake pushed their bikes over to us.

"This is intense," Phoenix said.

"No doubt," Jake said. "We're going to get slaughtered."

"Speak for yourself," Hú Dié said. "I am having a *great* time. I am not afraid."

"You're a girl," Jake said. "In fact, you're the *only* girl. They're going to take it easy on you."

"Then it will be their downfall."

My mom laughed. "Hú Dié is right. Her being the only

girl may be to your advantage. They might underestimate all of you because you're all dressed alike and hanging out together. You're clearly teammates."

"I think they're already underestimating us," Phoenix said. "I kind of thought we'd be mini celebrities, but these guys aren't even looking at us."

"So much the better," my mom said. "It's the sponsors you want the attention from, anyway, not the other riders."

"Sponsors?" Jake said. "Where?"

"Everywhere," my mom replied. "I saw their names when I signed you in. A few of them even approached me."

"Really?" I said.

"Really," my mom said, "but that's all I'm going to say until after the race. I wasn't going to mention it at all, but it sounds like you could use a little boost. Don't worry about the other riders. Just stick together and work as a team. You'll do well. I promise."

"Hello, Mystery Teen Team!"

I turned to see DuSow heading toward us with his riders in tow: Philippe, Lucas, and, unbelievably, SaYui. He'd somehow survived being shot by Bo. DuSow wore a bright orange rain suit, while Philippe, Lucas, and SaYui were decked out in riding gear and pushing their bikes. None of the riders had any visible injuries. Even Lucas's arm had healed. Apparently, the synthetic dragon bone worked.

DuSow must have seen me looking for signs of their previous wounds. "Everyone is one hundred percent," he said, "except Lin Tan, who is perhaps seventy-five percent healed. However, he isn't scheduled to race. He prefers to lie low, you know."

"I know," I said, glancing around. "Where's Peter?"

"Ah, yes. Your coach. He's a little . . . tied up at the moment. He won't be joining us."

I scowled. "You're going to make us wait until after the race to see him?"

DuSow laughed. "You're going to be waiting longer than that." He lowered his voice. "Your friend from Texas having killed my doctor set my program behind. I've yet to find a suitable replacement. I've spent too much time keeping the police away and making up stories for all the gunshots people heard the other night. Peter will be staying with us awhile longer."

"But that wasn't the deal!" I growled.

"Listen to you roar, little lion. You are more than welcome to find me after the race." He wiggled the fingers of his right hand at me.

I ground my teeth.

"Ladies and gentlemen!" someone announced with a bullhorn. *"It's time to get this party started!"*

DuSow winked at me and left.

My mother shook her head. "I take it that was Mr. Poison Hand."

"Yeah," I said.

"I don't believe that idiot!" Jake said. "What are we going to do?"

"Nothing for at least an hour," my mother said. "Forget about what he said for now. We'll get Peter back. Just focus on the race. If your attention wavers for an instant, you're going to be in big trouble."

I shook my head. "I can't forget."

"You have to," she said. "Now, I need to go over to the spectator area. I'll meet you at the finish line when you're through." She wished Phoenix, Hú Dié, and Jake good luck and then, to my horror, she leaned over and kissed my cheek before leaving the starting area.

I felt my face begin to burn with anger as well as embarrassment. At least the cool rain kept me from blushing. We lined up, and I wiped rainwater from my eyes. It felt a lot like tears. However, crying was the last thing on my mind. Revenge for Peter was all I could think about. My *dan tien* began to quiver, as though encouraging me to get off of my bike, find DuSow, and strangle him.

I took a deep breath and flipped on the handlebar-mounted light that Hú Dié had installed on each of our bikes. Phoenix said something, and so did Jake, but I didn't hear a word either one had said. In fact, I hardly even heard the starter pistol when it fired.

CRACK!

The starter pistol sounded a lot like Bo's rifle, which snapped me out of my daze. Riders began to hammer, and I hadn't even clipped my feet into my pedals yet.

"Ryan!" Jake shouted. "Get with the program, bro!"

I clipped in and blasted forward, my anger releasing itself through my legs. I nearly ran over the two guys directly in front of me. One of them said, "Geez, you sure can pound, kid!"

That should have given me hope about our chances to do well in the race, but I found that I no longer cared about it. All I cared about was Peter.

I'd gotten separated from Phoenix, Jake, and Hú Dié, and it took me half a lap of the hilly one-mile loop to work my way up to them. There were about fifty racers in all, and they were all excellent riders. We rode closer to one another than I thought possible. Whenever the guys around me would shake rain from their faces, it would hit me.

By the time I'd connected with the others, two different packs of four guys had broken away from the peloton.

"Want to make it three breakaways?" Hú Dié asked.

"Yeah!" Jake said.

"I'm game," Phoenix said. "Lead the way, Ryan."

My heart wasn't really into it, but I pushed forward anyway, signaling for the others to fall in behind me. I was already riding pretty hard, and I had to push myself almost to the breaking point to pull us a noticeable distance ahead of the main peloton.

I put us fifty yards out, and I glanced down at my electronic display. It showed thirty-eight miles per hour.

And we were on a straightaway.

We reached a downhill run, and I saw the two breakaway groups riding neck and neck about seventy yards ahead.

What the heck? I thought, and I began to hammer down the dark, wet hill.

"Ryan!" Phoenix shouted. "Slow down!"

I ignored him and glanced beyond the breakaway riders. I saw San Francisco Bay, and I was able to single out DuSow's docks. My heart nearly stopped. Tied up to one of the docks was a boat.

Peter, I thought. *How can I continue to ride when he is so close by?*

"Ryan!" Phoenix shouted again. *"Slow down!"*

I turned my gaze back to the breakaway groups and saw

that I was nearly upon them. I glanced down at my electronic display.

Sixty-one miles per hour.

Wet brakes squealed ahead of me, and I tickled my brake levers. It had little effect.

I did it again, and again, and again, drying them off. Finally, I began to slow. The breakaway riders made the next turn, and I cut my wheel to follow. I'd forgotten about how the wet pavement might affect my bike's shortened wheelbase and nearly cut the wheel too far. I straightened it out a bit and swerved onto the next street.

"Easy," Hú Dié huffed as she locked onto my rear wheel.

"Sorry," I said. "I wasn't paying attention."

"You'd better start!" Phoenix barked. "Don't take another hill at that speed again, or you'll be riding without us."

"Got it," I said.

The two breakaway packs had merged into one, and we caught up with them as we reached the start/finish line, marking the end of our first lap. We blasted past the crowd huddled in the rainy darkness, and they cheered. A few even rang cowbells. I saw my mom jumping up and down excitedly, and of course, DuSow's orange rain suit stood out like a sore thumb.

Once we were clear of the crowd, a rider cut out from the center of our twelve-man breakaway peloton and veered toward me. It was Lucas, and he was smiling like he had a secret. Before I could react, he lifted his leg exactly like Hú Dié had taught me for a side kick, and let fly. The perfect kick struck me in the hip, causing me to weave uncontrollably.

I began to lose traction and speed, and the next thing I knew, Hú Dié was beside me. She grabbed my handlebars, straightening me out and holding me steady as if I were a five-year-old riding without training wheels.

"Are you good?" she shouted.

"Yeah!" I shouted back.

She let go of my handlebars, and Phoenix and Jake pulled around me, forming a wall to protect me from further attack.

"That was Savat!" Hú Dié shouted. "A French martial art! Lots of kicks! Be careful around that guy!"

I nodded again.

"Are you okay?" she asked.

"Sure," I said.

But I could tell that Hú Dié knew as well as I did that I was anything but okay. My head just wasn't in the race. I needed to pull out before I hurt myself or, even worse, someone else.

I looked ahead and caught a glimpse of DuSow's warehouse again, and I couldn't take it anymore.

I shouted to Hú Dié, "I'm out! You're going to have to pull the team from here."

She looked concerned. "Dragon . . . you know?"

"No," I said. "Mechanical failure."

"Huh?"

"Falling off!" I shouted, and I pulled out of line. I rose up out of my saddle and hammered with all my might. At the same time, I wrenched my gearshift all the way down. My chain skipped and began to flap, skittering over the rear wheel's gear sprockets. I wrenched the gearshift all the way back up, and the chain suddenly caught. The transition from floppy and loose to guitar-string taut was too much.

SNAP!

My chain broke just like I'd experienced weeks ago on my mountain bike in Indiana. Except this time, I was ready for it.

I stopped pedaling as I swerved even farther to the side. Phoenix shot me a questioning glance, while Jake shouted, "We'll win this thing for you, bro!"

And then they were gone.

I pulled onto a dark side street as the main peloton rocketed past. I was panting like a dog, trying to catch my breath. I always seemed to be more winded when I stopped than when I was riding.

I climbed off of my bike and saw that the chain had managed to wrap itself around my drive sprocket, so I freed it. I took a quick look at the chain in my bike's light and found that the chain hadn't broken, after all. The quick-release master link had simply popped open. I closed it back up, repositioned the chain, and hit the road again, heading for DuSow's warehouse. I needed to get to Peter before the race finished and before DuSow realized I was gone.

I steered through the rainy darkness and caught a downhill slope toward the waterfront. I rode fast without encountering a single car or pedestrian to slow my progress, arriving in DuSow's brightly lit warehouse parking lot. I zipped around the building to the dock and felt a jolt of excitement as I read the name on the back of the boat: THE STRONG HOLD.

I slowed and heard a splashing sound from the direction of the building.

I turned to see DaXing running toward me, sloshing across the pavement. I tried to veer away, but the ground was too slick. I went down.

I managed to kick myself free of the bike and pop onto my feet before he was on me. I dropped into a low Horse Stance and raised my right knee to my chest. Then I thrust the ball of my foot toward his liver with a powerful front kick. He was agile for such a large guy, and he twisted to one side, avoiding my kick and retaliating with a round-house kick of his own.

This was the same kick Hú Dié had taught me to catch, so I raised my arm and let his leg connect with my rib cage, just below my armpit.

Big mistake.

CRUNCH!

I thought I felt a couple of ribs crack, and what little air my tired lungs had managed to collect was forced out of my mouth. My body went into autopilot, though, and I completed the sequence of moves I'd practiced a few thousand times with Hú Dié. My arm wrapped around DaXing's thick leg, and I took a giant step backward.

DaXing hit the ground. I released his leg and jumped onto his chest. My *dan tien* began to vibrate uncontrollably, and I formed hammer fists with my hands. I rained blow after blow on his face, head, and throat until he stopped moving.

I climbed off of him and watched his chest. He was still breathing. I was glad.

I hugged my aching side and ran over to the dock. There didn't seem to be a captain or anyone else aboard, but I was hopeful that Peter was somewhere inside. The boat rose and fell steadily, and I got the rhythm down before jumping onto the back deck. I didn't know a thing about boats, but this one didn't seem too large. I headed to an enclosed cabin, but when I reached to grab the doorknob, the door flew open.

Lin Tan stepped out into the rain holding a large pistol. Clean bandages crisscrossed his otherwise bare torso.

"Fancy seeing you here, Ryan," he said. "Why aren't you racing? Couldn't handle the heat, so you had to get out of the kitchen?"

"No," I replied. "I couldn't focus on crushing a bunch of riders, so I came here to crush you."

"Very funny." He pointed the gun at me, and I watched it bob up and down as the boat bobbed with the current.

Up.

Down.

Up.

I slammed the heel of my palm into Lin Tan's gun-hand wrist. The pistol flew from his hand, into the bay.

"Why you little . . . ," he said, and he swung a fist at my face.

I spun sideways and lifted my arm to deflect the blow. His fist hit my forearm, and my forearm hit the side of my head. I saw stars, but I didn't go down.

Lin Tan stepped in close to me, and I responded with the only close-distance move I knew. I raised my right knee and stomped my reinforced shoe into the side of Lin Tan's left kneecap with a knee-trap kick.

He wailed and teetered sideways, and I pounded hammer fists onto the bridge of his nose until it erupted with a crimson bloom that covered both of us. His eyes crossed, and he stumbled toward the boat deck railing and the dock beyond. He gripped the railing, then slumped, unconscious, with half of his body in the boat and the other half draped over the railing.

I ran into the cabin and found Peter bound to a kitchen chair that had been screwed to the floor. He was gagged, and his arms and legs were tied, but he was alert. He nodded to his left, and I saw a small galley counter. I opened a drawer beside the sink and found a large knife; then I cut Peter free.

"Thank you," Peter said with a sigh.

"No, thank *you*," I replied. "Do you have wheels?"

He shook his head. "No, but I don't need them."

Peter dropped out of the chair and began to army-crawl toward the door. I hurried ahead of him to hold the door open and froze.

On the dock was DuSow.

DuSow stood alone in the rain, the light of the warehouse's new security flood lamps illuminating him and the dock. I glanced back at Peter. "DuSow is out there!"

DuSow laughed. "All aboard!"

I stepped back into the cabin and closed the door, fumbling for the lock.

"No use," Peter said. "It's DuSow's boat. He has a key."

"Can we block the door with something?" I asked.

"It's a boat, Ryan. All the furniture is nailed down."

I grabbed the large knife I'd used to cut Peter free and flung the door back open, ready for DuSow. But he wasn't there. He was at the side of the deck, examining the still-unconscious Lin Tan's shattered nose.

"You did this?" DuSow asked.

"Yeah," I said.

"Impressive. Want to try to do that to mine?"

"No. I just want to leave with Peter."

"I thought as much. When I noticed that you weren't with the other riders, I got suspicious and came here. I'm missing the race because of you. That disappoints me." He removed his right glove. "It appears Lin Tan has disappointed me, too."

DuSow placed his right hand on Lin Tan's broken face, and Lin Tan began to shiver and shake, and then he went still.

I raised the knife. "Back off. I'm warning you."

DuSow snickered and stepped over Lin Tan. In a blur, he kicked the knife out of my hand.

My eyes widened. I couldn't believe he moved so fast. It had to be the dragon bone.

He removed his other glove and took a step toward me, and I saw him stumble. At first I thought it might be the slick deck, but then I noticed Peter's arm. He'd reached through the doorway and had grabbed DuSow's pant leg. DuSow leaned down to grab Peter's bare wrist.

"Peter! Let go!" I shouted. "Don't let him touch you!"

Peter didn't let go. Instead, he jerked his massive arm sideways, and DuSow hit the deck.

I tried to soccer-kick DuSow's head, but he was too quick. He rolled away, breaking Peter's hold. Peter army-crawled onto the deck and over to the railing. He began to pull himself up as DuSow stood.

I heard an engine roar, and out of the corner of my eye I saw a speedboat approaching at high speed. I thought it might be one of DuSow's associates, but the driver, some random jerk, never slowed. He cut the steering wheel an instant before colliding with us, and I heard a chorus of laughter beneath the boat's protective awning as someone called out, "Since you guys seem to like playing in the rain so much, here's some more water!"

A huge rooster tail washed over the deck, knocking me to my knees. The boat heaved from side to side, and I heard Peter shout, "Ryan!"

SPLASH!

He'd fallen overboard.

DuSow rushed toward me with the fingers of his deadly right hand splayed. I stood and made a move to leap over the railing after Peter, but I slipped and fell. I landed on my back, and as DuSow neared, I grabbed his foot firmly with both of my hands. I rolled backward, and as DuSow began to fall, I wrapped both of my legs around his one leg. His foot was still locked in my hands, and as he crashed to the deck, I clamped my legs together and twisted his foot in a complete circle like Hú Dié had taught me.

CRUNCH!

DuSow howled in pain, and I let go, jumping to my feet. I scrambled clear of his deadly hands and hopped the railing, onto the dock.

"Peter!" I shouted.

"Down . . . here!" he replied, sputtering.

I peered down and saw him treading water beneath the dock. He had a dangling dock line in one hand.

"The current is strong, but I'm fine," Peter said. "Do what you have to do!"

I looked back to the boat to see DuSow climb over the railing, onto the dock. He limped toward me, his foot dragging.

I turned to run and slammed straight into DaXing's gigantic chest. He smothered me with a bear hug, lifting me clear off the ground. I kicked and writhed and beat my forehead against his sternum, but it was no use. Most of my face was smashed up against his heavy raincoat, making it difficult for me to breathe. I managed to twist my head to one side, and I saw DuSow hobble up to us.

No one moved.

"What happened to your face?" DuSow asked DaXing.

DaXing didn't reply.

"What are you waiting for?" DuSow said. "Finish him, you big ape!"

"*You* finish him," DaXing said. "He's only a kid."

DuSow shook his head and closed the gap between us. He raised his hands, and DaXing suddenly flung me to the dock. He gripped DuSow's neck between his mighty hands, and I saw that DaXing was wearing heavy rubber gloves that went all the way up to his elbows.

DuSow choked once, and his face instantly turned blue. He raised his hands and grabbed DaXing's wrists, but his poisons had no effect through the rubber. DuSow began to kick DaXing and beat on the giant's arms, but DaXing didn't release his grip. In fact, it looked as if he began to squeeze tighter. Within a few moments, DuSow's arms hung limp at his sides and his eyes began to bulge.

I turned away. No amount of dragon bone was going to help him. I heard the thump as DaXing dropped DuSow to the dock, and I turned back.

"Thank you," I muttered.

"He had it coming," DaXing said. "Remember the man he killed the first time you saw me?"

"The guy with the panther tattoos?"

"Yes. DuSow said, 'Take your failure of a friend with you and dispose of his body.' Panther was more than my friend. He was my cousin. Let's help yours."

I hurried to the dock's edge, half expecting Peter to have hauled himself up, but he hadn't. He was still in the water. He wasn't holding the dock line, either. He'd tied it around his upper body.

"Peter!" I called down. "What's wrong?"

He didn't answer.

DaXing joined me and stared down at Peter. "Help me with the rope," he said.

DaXing began to haul the rope up, groaning under the strain of Peter's dead weight. I helped as much as I could, and we soon got Peter onto the dock. He was barely conscious.

"You'll understand if I leave now?" DaXing said.

"Yeah," I said. "Thanks again."

DaXing nodded and hurried off.

I knelt beside Peter.

"Thanks, Ryan," he mumbled.

"What's wrong?" I asked.

"My heart. The dragon bone. I—"

His voice trailed off.

A huge lump formed in my throat. "It's the dragon bone, isn't it?"

He nodded.

"And your heart hurts?"

"I have palpitations. I overheard Lin Tan and DuSow discussing the heart failure concerns they had. Swimming in the current and trying to climb that rope, I . . . over-exerted. I'm sorry."

I roared.

"Noooo!"

I jumped to my feet. There had to be something I could do! My *dan tien* quivered, and I remembered the dragon bone antidote. Would it work on the manufactured version?

"Hang on," I told Peter. "I have an idea."

I ran to my bike and grabbed my cell phone from the gear pouch beneath my seat. I shielded it from the rain as best I could and dialed Hok's number. She answered on the first ring.

"Hello?"

"Hok!" I said. "It's Ryan. We have an emergency."

"What is it?" she asked. "I'm watching the race. I noticed that you had dropped out. What happened?"

"I rescued Peter, only he overexerted himself. He's having heart palpitations! DuSow's manufactured dragon bone still doesn't work. We need to try the antidote. How fast can you get here?"

"I don't know, Ryan. Traffic is gridlocked around the entire race area because of the streets they've closed off. It's all over the news. I'd jog if I could, but I'm rather old for that."

"Wait!" I said. "My bike! I'll ride to your place, then ride back. I should be able to do it in time."

"We must try," Hok said. "You do not need to come all the way here. I can drive part of the way, or walk. Can you make it to Chinatown on your own?"

"I can get to the Dragon Gate."

"Perfect. I'll meet you there. Hurry, Ryan!"

I hung up the phone and climbed onto my bike. "I'll be back, Peter!" I screamed, and tore off into the night.

I raced along the waterfront, then up the extremely steep hill. My light cut a path through the rain, and I pushed myself to reach the top faster than I'd hoped. My body began to cramp, and my *dan tien* danced, but I shoved the pain aside and focused on Peter.

I heard a bullhorn siren wail for just a second, and then a chorus of cowbells rang out in the distance. The race was drawing to a close. It was the last thing on my mind.

After cresting the hill, I caught my first glimpse of the street. Bumper to bumper didn't even begin to describe the traffic. It was bumper *on* bumper. I veered onto the sidewalk and began to hammer between umbrella-toting pedestrians. Most of them saw me coming and leaped out of my way, but I had to shout at the more clueless ones.

The pavement was pockmarked and not all of the curbs had pedestrian ramps, so I did a lot of bunny hopping. I wished I'd had my 'cross bike or even my mountain bike, but I did what I could with my road bike, using my knees and elbows as shock absorbers. Miraculously, the bike and I made it to the Dragon Gate in one piece.

Hok was waiting for me.

"I can't believe you got here so quickly!" she said.

"Had to," I replied, sucking wind. "All my fault. Need to make it right."

"Not your fault," she said as she strapped a small backpack onto my back. "Give Peter one mouthful of the antidote. Now go!"

I spun my bike around and returned the way that I'd come, riding faster than before. I passed many of the same pedestrians for a second time, and they were even quicker to get out of my way.

It was also a straight downhill run for me when I reached the obnoxious hill. I'd be lying if I said that I wasn't looking forward to it. I hit sixty-five miles per hour before I finally tickled the wet brakes, and I was probably going thirty when I took the turn at the bottom.

I raced along the waterfront and made it back to Peter, who was now lying on the edge of the parking lot. I was overjoyed to find him still coherent.

"How did you get over here?" I asked.

"I crawled," Peter muttered. "I couldn't stand the sight of DuSow on the dock. Where did you go?"

"Hok developed an antidote for the dragon bone," I said, trying to catch my breath. "At least, it works with real dragon bone. No one has tried it with the manufactured version."

"Who is Hok?"

"YeeYee." I took off the backpack and removed a small

container of liquid. I unscrewed the cap and lifted Peter's head as I'd seen Hok do with Lin Tan. "Drink only one mouthful."

Peter wrinkled his nose. "What's that smell?"

"Dehydrated flying lizard. Just drink it."

Peter looked at me sideways, then swallowed a mouthful. I had to jerk the container away to prevent his convulsing body from knocking it out of my hands. I hung on to his head until the convulsing stopped and his upper body and arms curled into a tight ball.

Peter's body relaxed, and I heard him sigh.

"Peter?" I asked.

"Ryan . . . I think it worked." He smiled.

I smiled back.

A van suddenly rushed into the parking lot and skidded to a stop. My mother jumped out.

"Ryan! There you are! And Peter!"

She ran to my side as Phoenix, Hú Dié, and Jake jumped out of the van, followed by Lucas, Philippe, and SaYui.

What are they doing here? I wondered.

My mother glanced at DuSow's lifeless body, then back at me. "What on earth happened? I was looking everywhere for you!"

"I saved Peter," I said, standing. "Sorry I didn't give you a heads-up."

"Peter!" Hú Dié shouted. She knelt down and gave him a huge hug, while Jake and Phoenix leaned down and bumped fists with him.

Lucas looked at me, then nodded at DuSow, who was barely visible on the dock. "You?" he asked.

I shook my head, raindrops flying off my nose. "No. DaXing."

Lucas nodded again and turned to Philippe and SaYui. "Now we can die in peace."

"What are you talking about?" I asked.

"Heart palpitations," my mom answered. "All three of them. While I was frantically looking for you, I overheard them talking about it. They recalled your saying something once about them possibly dying from the dragon bone, and together we concluded that you might have come here to try to rescue Peter. They are terrified. They've apologized to Phoenix, Hú Dié, and Jake."

"And now to you," Lucas said. "I am sorry about that kick earlier. You deserve better. I apologize."

"As do I," Philippe said.

"And I," SaYui said.

Lucas turned to my mother. "Thank you for the ride. We should go inside and call the authorities about this before it is too late for us."

I tried to remember how much dragon bone antidote Hok had told me was left. *Four doses? Five? Peter has already taken one dose. . . .*

I decided it didn't matter. "Wait!" I said, holding out the container. "I have an antidote."

"*Quoi?*" Philippe asked. "Is this true?"

"It is," Peter said. "I experienced heart palpitations, too, and I just took the antidote. The dragon bone inside me is dead. I am certain."

"May we?" Lucas asked.

"Of course," I said. "There should be enough for all three of you."

"*Merci!*" Lucas said. "Thank you!" He reached out for the container.

"You guys better lie down first," I said.

All three of them lay down in the rain-soaked parking lot.

"Only drink one swallow," I said, "Lucas, you'll go first. Mom, hold his head? He's going to shake."

"Sure," my mom said, and she knelt next to Lucas.

I handed him the container, and he took a drink. I snatched it back from him, though, as he began to tremble and go through the same sequence Peter had. When it was over, he passed out. However, his breathing was regular. He appeared to be fine.

I turned to Philippe and SaYui.

"Do you still want it?" I asked.

They both nodded.

"Phoenix, Hú Dié," I said. "Could you please hold their heads like my mom did?"

Phoenix and Hú Dié knelt down, and I gave one dose each to Philippe and SaYui. As their bodies went through the traumatic routine and Phoenix and Hú Dié held them, I glanced into the container.

There was still one dose left.

I looked over at my mom and saw that she was staring at me. She knew what I was thinking.

"Go ahead, if you want," she said. "I'll hold you."

I didn't know what to do. I wanted dragon bone out of my life, but drinking poison was a huge risk.

I could wait and take it some other time . . . , I thought.

Suddenly, as if taunting me, my *dan tien* quivered.

That did it.

I walked over to my mom and lay down next to her in the rain.

She kissed my cheek. "Are you sure?"

"Positive," I said.

"I am proud of you, Ryan."

I smiled. "I'm proud of me, too."

She took my head in her hands, and I lifted the container to my lips, downing the last of the antidote.

I remember twitching and shaking and feeling as though my insides were being ripped apart. I also remember my mom holding me tightly, telling me everything was going to be all right.

But more than anything, I remember Jake's voice saying, "Crap! I forgot to tell him that I won!"

About the Author

Jeff Stone is the author of the hugely successful Five Ancestors books. When that series concluded, he wanted to write something different from another tale set in seventeenth-century China. However, he was reluctant to completely let go of kung fu or the characters he had grown to love, so he created a new series to update them to his own time. Jeff lives in Indiana with his wife and two children, and while he's active in several forms of bike racing, mountain biking is his favorite. Jeff has been to San Francisco's Chinatown many times, but he has yet to meet any four-hundred-year-old apothecaries. (At least, that's what he tells people.)

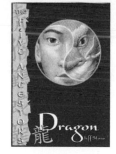